AT SUCH CLOSE RANGE they could clearly hear the bullets slapping into the man's body. Dzhombe, favored of the gods and inheritor of the Kingdom of Shaka, rolled back up from the floor to his feet. He quivered for a moment, then shook his body, whipping a spray of sweat and blood all over the room.

"Fools," he gurgled. The gaping holes in his chest and back seemed not to give him any pain at all.

"Fools, you cannot kill me. Only the gods have that right. I am their child, Shaka, born again into the body of Matthew Dzhombe!"

Charter Books by Barry Sadler

CASCA:

THE AFRICAN MERCENARY

BARRY SADLER

#12

CHARTER BOOKS, NEW YORK

CASCA: THE AFRICAN MERCENARY

A Charter Book / published by arrangement with
the author

PRINTING HISTORY
Charter Original / October 1984

ISBN: 0-441-09260-8

Charter Books are published by The Berkley Publishing Group,
200 Madison Avenue, New York, New York 10016.
PRINTED IN THE UNITED STATES OF AMERICA

Julius Goldman, M.D.
Boston, Mass.

My dear Landries:

Continuing to live up to my promise to let you have first look at the Casca manuscripts, I enclose the latest episode. After the release of *Soldier of Fortune*, I have been besieged by letters wanting to know more about our friend's contemporary adventures. To that effect, I hope that this will suffice.

For obvious reasons, some of the names of the principals and places have been changed. As to the person Matthew Dzhombe, his ultimate fate was never referred to as made public, and many sources believe he is living in exile in a friendly country in North Africa.

It was most difficult to contact our friend this time. As you will see, he suffered many losses in this adventure and, like most wounded creatures, will need some time by himself to heal.

I, myself, sometimes grow very weary. Through his story, I quite often feel that I am losing my own identity and am being absorbed by his incredible odyssey. It is through this, my long association with him, that I understand his wish for eternal peace. It may seem strange, but I often find myself wishing he would receive that which he wishes most—to die, to sleep, perchance to dream. . . .

As Casca Rufio Longinus would say,

Eternally yours,

Julius Goldman, M.D.

CHAPTER ONE

Outside of Bern, Switzerland, in a storybook château overlooking a lake, ten men sat together, united only by their mutual mistrust. There were five white and five black Africans. On one side of the polished conference table sat the descendants of the Bantu tribesmen who had subjugated most of central Africa for centuries. On the other sat the heirs of the tough-minded Dutch settlers, the Boers, who had destroyed the Zulu nation and conquered that land for their own, building their cities and universities where once the kraals of the Mplele held sway over the veldt.

Beneath the formal courtesy of each group lay their

violent heritage. These men were going into a partnership out of necessity, not friendship. The black Africans were representatives of the insurgents wishing to take over the government of Matthew Dzhombe's Kimshaka. The whites were an island of sunburned faces surrounded by a hostile black ocean. They wanted a secure outlet to the sea to prevent their being completely cut off from the outside world in case of an embargo by the United Nations.

Understanding this, both groups—the blacks uncomfortable in ill-fitting suits, the whites sullen over having to deal with them—came to an agreement. The black Africans were among the few surviving members of Kimshaka's intelligencia, and had either been driven into exile or had managed to escape before Dzhombe's executioners found them. All had reasons for wanting to return. All had lost members of their families to the executioners, and all had friends still being held in concentration camps or, as His Excellency Matthew Dzhombe referred to them, "reeducation centers."

The negotiations had been going on for eleven days, both sides twisting and testing each and every word of their agreement until at last they had made their pact. If the Boers were successful in arranging the timely demise of Matthew Dzhombe, the new government would cede to the whites a narrow strip of land leading from their country through Kimshaka to the sea, giving the whites their corridor through which supplies could reach them without hindrance. Their country would no longer be isolated or subject to the whims of a madman. Before leaving, the white delegation made one more veiled threat, letting their unwilling black allies know that if they went back on their word, they would be the next ones to die.

Leaving the black Africans still sitting, the Boers returned to their consulate and sent a coded message confirming their agreement to their capital. The following day, the head of state security for their country, Colonel Alan van Janich, changed from his normal khaki drill uniform into a lightweight suit that did little to hide his military nature. The fact that he was a soldier was as obvious as if the words were tattooed on his brow. He had received his orders and had been told to go to the limits of his power to negotiate.

Van Janich knew where to go to find the hirelings he needed. Through one of his colleagues on Taiwan, a Major Shan, he had been put in touch with a man whom Shan had said was highly qualified for jobs that required a closed mouth and a quick mind. There was no shortage of mercenaries in Africa, but this job required special skills, and it would be best if the faces for this contract were not too well known. During that initial telephone call, Shan had given van Janich a briefing on a man called Casey Romain, whom the Chinese had used on a recent job in Cambodia. Shan was not personally fond of the man, but he assured the Boer that Mr. Romain always held up his end of a bargain. At van Janich's urging, Shan related what he knew of the mercenary's background. Casey was a former Foreign Legionnaire who had seen action in French Indochina and Algeria, and was a veteran of the United States' debacle in Vietnam. Shan had sent van Janich a recent photograph of Casey Romain, adding that he thought the man had also served in the German Wehrmacht. Van Janich found that hard to believe; the man in the photo, who had an ugly scar running from the corner of his eye to his mouth, looked to be no older than his mid-thirties.

Van Janich took a commercial flight to Johannesburg, and from there, with only a two-hour layover, he was on his way to Hong Kong with a stop at Bangkok. He hoped that everything would go as planned and that this special man, Casey Romain, would be waiting for him when he touched down. If he wasn't, then his timetable would be shot to hell and he'd have to start over, looking for someone else who had a death wish.

Van Janich was pleased to see that the face in the photograph Major Shan had sent him was waiting with the crowd gathered to greet the new arrivals to the British crown colony on the doorstep of Communist China. *My God!* he thought, and being a good member of the Dutch Reformed Church, he rarely used the Lord's name in vain. *That's one man I wouldn't want to have angry with me.* There was a latent power to the man, who, though of average size, had the thick body of a fighter and gave off an unmistakable message: "It would be best if you let me be." The mercenary's hands werre scarred, as was his face, and through the open collar of his khaki shirt, van Janich saw more evidence of past wounds. He had the uneasy feeling he would not like to see the man naked.

Van Janich's hand was shaken firmly but without undue pressure by powerful fingers. He was greeted, if not warmly, at least with a modicum of courtesy.

"Welcome to the Orient, Mr. van Janich," Casey said. The voice was not exceptional, only a bit strange in its texture. There was something in the intonation that was both familiar and alien at the same time. Well, Shan had warned him that Casey Romain was not your average hired killer. Refusing Casey's offer to take his briefcase, van Janich followed after the square back as it led the way through the throngs of people to a bar and cocktail lounge where passengers could watch the planes take off.

Van Janich found that Casey Romain already had a good idea of what the Boers wished him to undertake, so he just filled in the details over a few gin and tonics. Casey soon set his mind at ease, at least as far as his expertise in matters such as these were concerned. His questions were kept to a minimum, but all were vital and to the point. The Boer security officer sweated a bit more than usual, but his new acquaintance showed no signs of anxiety or tension. Van Janich couldn't put his finger on the man's attitude. It was as if what was being offered him really didn't matter at all. Van Janich felt that Casey was taking this contract to kill a man merely to use up time.

They reached a basic understanding before van Janich's flight to Tokyo departed three hours later. The number of men, the mission, and the pay were all agreed upon. Within a week, deposits would be made to the proper accounts in Zürich and Brussels. Once van Janich was certain Casey was his man, he gave him his briefcase. Inside was information necessary to begin operational planning: names of those for and against Matthew Dzhombe; photos, charts, maps, and timetables for trains, planes, and buses; the times of the tides; and a list of holidays in both the target area and the surrounding nations.

As the British-trained security officer left him to board the flight to Tokyo, Casey was already going over the list of his first priorities. He still had a couple of hours before his own flight left for Singapore. He moved to a corner booth in the lounge where the sounds of voices and laughter wouldn't interfere with his thinking. He was lost in his own thoughts and never noticed the obvious

invitation made by the attractive waitress who brought
him his drink. She left a bit disappointed that she wasn't
able to get at least a smile from the solidly built man
with the scarred face and tired blue-gray eyes.

At that moment, however, Casey Romain had more
pressing things on his mind than the interest and avail-
ability of the waitress. Sliding over in his booth to where
he could set his legs half on the cushions, he wondered
again, as he always did, who among his rapidly declining
number of acquaintances would be next to die. He wondered why he troubled himself with such futile speculation. It made no difference who died; others would
always be there to take their places. *Vive la mort! Vive
la guerre! Vive le mercenaire!*

Straightening up, he winced as a muscle knotted up
below his left shoulder blade. A round from a Czech-
made AK-47 had punched a neat puckered hole through
him there, a part of his built-in collection of souvenirs.
Like most of his profession, he carried his wartime mem-
ories on his body. Running a hand through short-cropped,
sandy hair, he hauled himself up out of the booth after
checking his Rolex. He had a lot to do, and time was
short.

Outside the lounge he checked on his flight. It was
on time and due to depart in thirty minutes to take him
back to Singapore, where in three days he would verify
the transfer of the monies he would need. While waiting,
he began to develop the timetable for his plans and review
the data that van Janich had given him about the current
situation in Kimshaka and the surrounding countries.

From what he had heard of Matthew Dzhombe, the
bastard needed killing, and there would be little mourning
for him even among his own tribesmen. He also knew

that whoever took over the government after Dzhombe's demise would not be much better. But that wasn't his problem. He was only a man paid to do a job.

CHAPTER TWO

Dust clouds rose over the dry lands to the west and south, whisked into the heated air of the African sky. The serenity of the heavens was being broken that day by repeated bursts of rifle fire in the courtyard of the presidential palace.

A shame, thought the massive form. *To be the Chosen One is hard. But my brothers should have known better, and if one chooses to oppose me, then he deserves his fate. It is the will of the gods.*

Matthew Dzhombe's life had been devoted to those dark gods of his youth in the tiny kraal deep in the bush country where the wizards of his village had passed him through the rituals of manhood and initiated him into the warrior society of his tribe.

He had seen men die and shrivel when the Holy Ones put the juju on them. He knew the power of the Unseen Ones, and in his mind they lived, alive and real! They had brought him to power and had told him who his enemies were, and Matthew Dzhombe, the Avenging Lion of Kimshaka, was afraid of them.

Sometimes at night they would come and punish him, showing him the unspeakable things that would be done to him if he did not obey them. He would obey and do whatever they wished. If he had to hurt his people, it was because he was ordered to, and when it was over, he knew that the gods were right. They were always right, because he always felt so good when it was done. One must never fight the will of the gods.

The troops below had finished their preparations. The sound of bolts closing on rifles was followed by the repeated chatter of automatic fire cutting down the figures tied to the stakes. There was a few seconds' pause, then the regularly spaced cracks of pistol shots as the officer in charge of the firing squad delivered the *coup de grace* with a single, well-placed bullet to the back of the head of each of the twenty-two men and women who had dared to offend the gods and their servant. When the sound of the last shot faded away, Dzhombe felt a warm glow of satisfaction spread throughout his body.

Moving to his desk of hand-carved ebony, Dzhombe sat, his two-hundred-and-eighty-pound frame remarkably similar to one of the mountain gorillas that lived to the northwest of Kimshaka. His eyes were small and dark, the lids red-rimmed. Tribal scars adorned his face like a series of well-laid railroad ties waiting for the tracks to be placed on them.

It had been necessary for him to remove from his census no less than 150,000 persons, most of them from tribes with whom his people had a long history of rivalry and intertribal warfare. Old hatreds die hard, and those learned in one's youth live the longest. Each foe eliminated made his role that much more secure. And while to the minds of the outside world there could be no doubt that Dzhombe was insane, he was still in power. Within him ran a streak of shrewdness and the innate ability to anticipate his enemy's actions. Matthew Dzhombe was a dangerous man.

The first thing he did upon seizing power, in the coup he had precipitated fifteen years earlier, was to have all the whites and mixed bloods, including Asians, Arabs, and anyone else not a black African, relocated and held until he decided what the best method of disposing of them would be. If he'd had his choice in the matter, the solution would have been obvious. But once he'd assumed the reins of power, he had to make some small concessions to the outside world, for there were many things he needed that could only come from either the East or West, mostly the weapons necessary to keep him in power.

He sighed with regret. It would have been so much easier if he had been able to simply line them all up and let his Simbas chop them to pieces with their long spears, the assegais. Whites were especially dangerous to him; they were too educated. He didn't trust people with too much education; they were always troublemakers, especially the missionaries. Those people had some insane compulsion to change the customs of centuries by teaching the tribesmen to read and write, causing them to become dissatisfied with their existence. Then they offered their pale, pathetic Jesus as an insipid substitute for their own vital lords of nature. It was their teachings that caused most of his problems at the country's single university located in his capital. They encouraged the students to start trouble. But he had seen films from Europe and America, and saw the problems the industrialized west had with its young people. He was going to make sure that would not happen in Kimshaka.

One out of every three college graduates was dead. Every missionary, if not dead, had been deported along with every foreign landowner. He hated letting most of them go, but he did feel some satisfaction when he had four young whites executed for possession of narcotics. The United Nations did nothing. True, he had received a letter of protest from some U.N. office professing concern about possible violation of the human rights of those who had been executed or jailed.

Dzhombe chuckled, his belly shaking at the thought of written protests. For the United Nations to say they thought he had acted in an overly harsh manner was hardly an intimidating indictment. All it proved to him was that the West would do nothing, especially once he had let the Russians move in and outfit his army. The Russians were a little more difficult to deal with, but not much. They wanted a toehold in central Africa so badly, they would believe almost anything and give nearly everything to get it. He gave them enough time to train his army and equip it with new modern weapons. The Russians thought they had him in their pocket, but before the Soviets could convert too many of his people into their agents, he had turned his secret police—the ones they had trained so expertly!—loose on them and their few supporters.

For executing the leftist subversives and expelling the Soviets, who were obviously interfering in Kimshaka's domestic affairs and fomenting disorder, the West had applauded him and then immediately offered to take the Soviet Union's place. Dzhombe let them and took them the same way he had taken the Russians, then ran them out of the country once he got what he wanted from them.

The American secretary of state said that he thought the premier of Kimshaka had acted in bad faith, another condemnation from the West that did not upset Dzhombe terribly. However, by using the money, weapons, and training given his country by both the East *and* West, Dzhombe had all the opposition he could find, real or imagined.

Dzhombe liked to think he was color-blind. He had the thirty or so black Americans in his country expelled along with the rest of the American advisors. He had more sense than to want those troublemakers loose in his country. Besides which, they were the descendants of slaves and were not true Africans no matter how much they tried to pretend they were.

Dzhombe had sent all of the Americans packing except for three he had killed himself while questioning them. The American State Department had accepted without question the story that they had been killed by Marxist insurgents.

Matthew Dzhombe, premier for life by his own de-cree, was quite satisfied with himself as he sat in his office. Only one group was in any way opposing him, the National Front for the Liberation of Kimshaka—the N.F.L.K. It was, for the most part, a loose alliance of members of the southern tribes of the desert and outer regions of the country who were being given aid by the colonialist whites who occupied what he rightly felt should be his land.

He would attend to that white country in time, but at present they gave him no trouble. He had them land-locked, and the closest route to the sea was controlled by him. As long as they paid his price, he would continue to let vital materials get through to them by way of Kimshaka's one operating rail line. He had a stranglehold on them, and he had no fear that they would try to invade and take the rail line by force. The United States and its ambassador to the U.N., the black activist George Old-erman, would see to that. All Dzhombe had to take care of was the N.F.L.K., and as long as they spent most of their time in Angola, he really didn't give a damn about them. And, he figured, they could always provide him with an excuse to remove anyone he considered to be bothersome by merely declaring them to be supporters of the traitors.

Matthew Dzhombe felt he had done well. He had his army, the wealth of his country's resources, and a very healthy Swiss bank account at his disposal, eight sons—one didn't count girl children—and of course he had the gods on his side to counsel and protect him. Soon it would be time for him to make his annual pilgrimage to the village of his birth. For a short time he would return to the old ways. He would sit in the huts of those who belonged to his clan, and in secret places known only to them, sacrifices would be made to the primal forces of creation as they had been made since the heavens and earth had been formed from the skull of a hippopotamus.

CHAPTER THREE

In Singapore, Casey sat with his number one man, a Vietnamese named Van, in the cool interior of Raffles, one of the last vestiges of the British Empire's better days. Van had been of great value to him on more than one occasion because of the man's family connections on Taiwan. Members of his once very large family had been in nearly every branch of the overthrown South Vietnamese government, and through them Van had many contacts with friendly interests on Taiwan. Van had a sleepy look to him that was deceptive. His smooth good looks and fine olive skin made many who saw him from even a short distance mistake him for Spanish or Portuguese.

Casey leaned back, listening to the drone of the over-worked air-conditioning system, sipping slowly at his *stengah,* enjoying the blend of whiskey and soda. Van was savoring both his San Miguel beer and the pretty Malay waitress, whose blue and white cheongsam showed a sleek length of golden leg where the dress was slit to the thigh.

Waiting was not all that bad. Van Janich had lived up to the letter of their agreement and had deposited the money into Casey's accounts in Brussels and Zürich. His machinery had been put into operation, and everything was in order. For once, he wouldn't have to go to the trouble of acquiring weapons. Working through the diplomatic pouches of the Boer's legation in Singapore, he had a direct line by which to send and receive information with little likelihood of a leak being made either accidentally or on purpose. He'd sent van Janich a list of his needs through the pouch and had been assured that the contractors would have everything he'd requested ready for him and his men at the staging area.

Casey signaled for a refill. "Not long now," he mumbled to Van, who just nodded his head and wondered if the girl was wearing panties under the liquid silk dress that slid over her hips like the skin of a snake when she walked. "Not long now," he repeated to himself.

The rest of the team would be flying in from Bangkok on Garuda, the Indonesian airline. Gustaf Beidemann, the German, had requested a couple of days layover in Thailand to visit some friends before meeting with Casey. If it had been anyone else, Casey would have told him to get his ass in gear, but he knew Beidemann would have just told him to piss off, and then would go ahead and do what he wanted to anyway. There was no way to ever completely control Beidemann; he'd given up trying a long time ago. It had been several years since he'd last seen his old comrade. They had been through much together since the fall of the Third Reich: the Legion in Indochina, Dien Bien Phu, then back to Algeria for the troubles there. In those days Casey had gone by the name of Carl Langers, the same one he'd used as a panzer soldier. It had become a bit too well known since then, and when he'd received his discharge from the French Foreign Legion, he had taken the name Casey Romain. Beidemann still had a hard time remembering not to call him Langers. The other man with Beidemann was his sidekick, a swarthy Moroccan he'd tied up with in Algeria in '57. He was known as Ali ben Yousef, and had a propensity toward the use of the knife and garrote.

They had all worked together before, and each knew the others' strong points and weaknesses. They were a good solid team. Casey forced his mind to leave the job alone. There wasn't anything else he could do right now. Too much thinking too early and he'd get edgy. There would be plenty of time to get worked up once they were on their way.

Van was about to go and take a leak, but before he stood up, a shadow filled the room, a silhouette in the doorway against the bright sunlight as it cased the bar.

Van nudged Casey's foot. Another, smaller silhouette joined the first. The figures were dimly lit, but the size of the first one left no doubt that it was Gustaf Beidemann, formerly of the French Foreign Legion, the Twenty-Seventh Panzer Division, and a half-dozen other outfits of one kind or another.

Beidemann could get by in several languages that he'd learned solely for the purposes of buying women or ordering a drink. And he suffered from one great weakness: a passion for Russian vodka. When it was available, he would consume it by the liter, saying it was the only damned thing Russia had worth going to war over.

The smaller figure beside him was Ali ben Yousef, a wiry little guy with the ability to open up a man faster than most could even think about it. His only loyalty was to Beidemann. The German had saved the little Moroccan's life once, and Yousef, being a devout Moslem, believed it was a sign from Allah. He'd vowed to serve the big man until the moment Allah—in His infinite wisdom and mercy—let him know the debt was paid off. And if and when that time came, Yousef hadn't quite made up his mind whether he would kill Beidemann or not. But such things were in the hands of Allah, blessed be His name. *Imshallah!*

Beidemann pulled a chair over to Casey's table while Yousef watched the door. Ordering a beer from the now meek waitress, who seemed awed by the dimensions of her new customer, he smiled at Casey. Speaking in clipped but correct English, he spoke in that slightly superior tone that so many Germans and upper-class Englishmen seem to acquire at about the same moment they reach puberty. In Beidemann's case, however, it had taken forty years longer. Casey was amused at his friend's attempt at sophistication.

"Carl, old friend, what is it that you want from these tired old bones that you should bring me all the way from Munich? It must be something of importance. Don't you realize Oktoberfest will be starting soon?"

Casey grinned back. "Gustaf, you old Hun, I brought you here because I have found that in spite of all my past experiences with you, I once more need you with me. I have a nice contract, one which will enable you to open your own restaurant where you can eat and drink to the end of your days, and never have to tip the waiter to get a good table. Now be still and listen. This is the situation . . ."

As Casey explained, Van moved over to the bar to talk with the waitress, keeping her out of earshot of the two men's conversation. Casey and Beidemann huddled together, heads nearly touching as Casey went over the basics of the operation and the problems concerning completion of the license.

As Beidemann was reading the reports given to Casey by van Janich, Casey couldn't help thinking about the monster sitting across from him. Beidemann was the last survivor of their original crew in Russia. They'd fought together in Indochina and Algeria while with the Second Parachute Battalion of the French Foreign Legion. There had been a couple of other small contracts since then. Casey had contacted him, and Beidemann hadn't turned down any of them. Van was not particularly fond of Beidemann, thinking him to be some kind of throwback to a more primitive form of mankind, one that should have disappeared with Peking Man.

The only member of Casey's crew to accept Beidemann totally was Ksor Tonn, better known as George, a Montagnard from the central highlands of Vietnam who was now back at Casey's plantation in Malaya. He'd be coming to Singapore tomorrow. George thought Beidemann was perfectly normal, except for his being six-feet-six and weighing as much as a pregnant water buffalo. Other than that, George accepted Beidemann as an equal.

Beidemann had picked up Yousef while in Algeria twelve years earlier, and the little Moroccan had been with him ever since. Over the years, Beidemann had come to hold a strange kind of affection and respect for his uninvited shadow.

If it had been anyone other than Casey Romain who had called him at this time, he probably wouldn't have come. He and Yousef were nearly set up with a contract to train the troops of one of the Persian Gulf emirates. The emir was a reasonable man who appreciated the finer things in life and wanted those in his service to do the same. Consequently, there would have been an abundance of lovely maidens and a constant flow of the best beer and vodka. It was with some reluctance that Beidemann had asked for a delay before entering the emir's service.

Once Beidemann had finished reading van Janich's reports, Casey gave him a quick rundown on how he thought they might be able to fulfill the contract. After listening to Casey's ideas, Beidemann stopped him with a raised hand. "You want to parachute into the palace grounds of Matthew Dzhombe?" He let loose a long, worried sigh. "That, my friend, may present more difficulties than you realize. It is one thing to get on the grounds; it is another thing entirely to be able to get out again—at least under your own power. Most of the black soldiers in that part of Africa aren't worth the price of the bullets it takes to kill them, but these Simbas of Dzhombe's are a different matter. I served with men of their tribe during the Katanga mess. Those men will run twenty miles to get in a fight, then will eat the livers of the still living bodies of any prisoners they take. It is not going to be easy. How many men will we have to do the job with?"

Casey took a long pull at his *stengah*, swallowing a

piece of ice that gave him a temporary burst of pain right between the eyes. He waited until the pain passed before answering.

"Fifty. Two twenty-man teams and a heavy weapons unit of ten men with two mortars and a recoilless rifle. When we hit the palace, the bulk of the Simbas there will hopefully be drawn off to counterattacks made by the N.F.L.K. at some small outposts outside the city.

"There should be no more than a hundred soldiers left inside the palace grounds. We ought to be able to handle them with the surprise element working for us."

Biedemann nodded slowly. "It may be possible, but how are we to extricate ourselves from the city and the country after the hit is made?"

Casey smiled. "By armored car and half-tracks, jeeps, whatever is available at the palace—taxis if we have to. According to the input I've received, there are several fully serviced vehicles kept on the palace grounds at all times. We take some of these and run for the bush country. The N.F.L.K. will be waiting on each of the routes out of the city to intercept us and provide us with security until we can get to the pickup site where the contractors will have a plane ready to fly us out.

"Each man will receive twenty-five thousand dollars for one day's work. You will get an extra ten for being the leader of one of the twenty-man squads. Is it agreed?"

"Agreed," said the old warrior. "Who is going to be in charge of the heavy weapons section?"

Casey inclined his head to where Van was obviously making an indecent proposal to the waitress in the tight cheongsam. "Van. Any objections?"

"None," said the graying giant. "Van is a good man and will be where he is needed the most. I think the only reason I let you talk me into these things is that I don't believe you could survive without the help of old Uncle Gus to take care of you as I have always done. Now, where are the others?"

Casey finished off the last of his *stengah* before answering. "At my plantation in Malaya. That's where we'll rehearse the operation and plan the final strike sequences."

"Good, good," said Beidemann and smiled broadly. "The more rehearsal we have, the more men will survive. How long do we have to prepare for the mission?"

Casey looked at his wristwatch calendar, though he already knew the answer. "We have four weeks. The only date we can be absolutely sure Dzhombe will be in the capital is on the anniversary of his taking power. In the last five years he has not missed making a Castro-style speech to the inhabitants. We hit him that night."

Beidemann ordered another round with a snap of his sausagelike fingers. "Two more questions, my friend. How large is the drop zone? And how do we know when we are over it?"

The questions were good ones and not unexpected. The German, like himself, had learned much with the Legion paratroopers. "The clearing we jump into is at the rear of the palace. It's about the size of a football or cricket field with some trees and brush, but it's not too bad. We'll know when to exit the aircraft by a radio signal preset by the N.F.L.K. If the weather is bad, they will have set up radio signals that will show up on the special direction finding equipment installed in the aircraft. The planes' DF will show a triangulation at the precise spot where we're supposed to jump. So we could jump blind if we had to. It won't make any difference if there's no moon or if there's ground fog; we jump on the radio signal." Casey waited to see if any of what he had just said needed any further explanation. It didn't, so he went on.

"There will be two sticks of jumpers, one in each plane. We can drop all the men in each stick in less than fifteen seconds. Using steerables, we can be fairly sure of everyone hitting the DZ with a minimum of error."

Beidemann nodded in satisfaction. "Good enough, old friend. If you say that's the way to do it, then I'm with you." He ended the question-and-answer session by raising his voice to a mild roar and calling Yousef and Van over to the table. He bellowed at the pretty waitress to get off her butt and bring drinks for all, and to make sure it went on Casey's bill. Trying to make up with Van, he gave the smaller Vietnamese a gentle, comradely slap on the shoulder, knocking Van off his chair to careen into a neighboring table. Beidemann's happy laughter startled a mule outside the door of the bar, causing the poor creature and its cart full of night soil meant for the rice paddies to bolt down the street. Its Chinese owner raced after the braying beast, hoping the animal's aged heart would not burst from the unexpected strain.

Laughing, Casey asked his huge friend, "Gus, where the hell did you learn to whisper? In a steel mill?"

"No," came the immediate response. "As you well know, it was in a Tiger tank on the Dnieper Line."

Fresh drinks were brought for all, and Van was helped back to his chair, though he did move it a bit farther away from the long, friendly reach of Beidemann. The old German soldier smiled benevolently at all present. "This is good. Besides which, the son of a bitch Dzhombe needs killing. It's always good to take on a job that rewards the soul as well as the purse. Now, enough of this talk! Let us drink and party tonight. And I, Gustaf Beidemann, former corporal by the will of God and a part-time house painter whose name escapes me at the moment, will teach you poor *Untermensch*—subhumans in English—how to really, as the Americans say, 'get down.'"

Another bottle of Stolichnaya vodka had him spending the rest of the evening trying to teach Van how to sing the marching songs of the Legion.

CHAPTER FOUR

Morning found Van, Casey, and Yousef trying to decide whether it was worth it to continue living. Van was in the john, doing his best to survive a case of the dry heaves, the kind that feels as if your stomach is doing its best to turn inside out and finally crawl out of your open mouth. Casey's eyes held a remarkable resemblance to two olives floating in a glass of stale tomato juice. The three men's states were further aggravated by the fact that Beidemann was doing his daily routine of push-ups and sit-ups. That, compounded by his singing something filthy about a girl named Lorelei, did nothing to make the day seem any more welcome.

While the others were trying to pull themselves together, Beidemann went down to the Telok basin to find some steak and fresh raw oysters for breakfast. Yousef was too ill to go with him and simply sat in a corner holding his head between his hands, repeating over and over that he now knew why Allah, in His infinite wisdom, prohibited the drinking of alcohol by the faithful, which he now swore to become. He promised to make a pilgrimage to Mecca and Medina if he lived through the rest of the day. Why had he been cursed with having to follow that monstrous barbarian around the world? What was his great sin that Allah should punish him so?

By noon, contrary to all expectations, Casey and the others discovered with a certain amount of amazement that they would survive. A few gallons of coffee later, plus some home remedies, and the worst was over.

Shortly after noon, Beidemann returned, belching contentedly and mumbling something to himself about how a few drinks at night aided the morning's digestive juices. Casey had to keep Van from throwing a butcher knife at the German's unsuspecting back.

It was with a sense of relief that Casey told Beidemann that he and Yousef would be going to the plantation in Malaya to start getting things laid out. Giving them each some pocket money—but not enough to party on—he told them to find the limey pilot, Harrison, who had a full-time girl friend not too far from the old Buddhist temple. He'd fly them over to Kuala Lumpur, and from there Beidemann and Yousef would have to take Casey's Land-Rover, which had been left at the airport, and drive on up to the cool beauty of the Cameron Highlands.

Beidemann asked if Casey's woman would be there. He had never met Yu Li, but he knew of her and how she and his old friend had come to be together. A Major Shan had contracted Casey to take some men and go into Cambodia to bring out a family of Chinese merchants that had been left behind when the Khmer Rouge took over. The mission had not gone down as smoothly as it should have. From the very beginning the Communists had been on their asses, and it had been a running fight all the way to the sea, where Yu Li's father had died when he exploded a can of gas in the hold of the pursuing Cambodian gunboat that had caught them. They had been sold out and knew who had done it. Beidemann had not been on that job, but he knew that whoever it was that had informed on Casey and his men would not go without his just reward.

Beidemann grumbled a bit when Casey told him to get his and Yousef's gear together and do as he was told. He finished his packing and, with one last wounded look before he left, asked, "Are you sure that we can't help?" He knew that their being sent on ahead had something to do with what had happened in Cambodia.

Van interjected with a terse, "No! This is our debt to pay! You were not there. This must be handled by us. It is a matter of honor." Accepting Van's statement, Beidemann bade them farewell and, with Yousef in tow, left the apartment for the streets below. He was attempting to hail a taxi when a voice called out his name.

George was getting out of a rickshaw. He had taken the morning shuttle from Kuala Lumpur. He had only met Beidemann once before, but that was enough; the giant was not easily forgotten. To Beidemann, the small Montagnard did not look all that well. He'd been wounded pretty badly during the Cambodian excursion with Casey, and it had taken months to get his strength back and to get used to his new artificial eye. Beidemann thought the effect of having one green eye and one brown quite striking, though he could see how it might be a bit disconcerting to the less sophisticated. Nevertheless, he thought it gave George a certain élan that went quite well with the gold teeth set with green plastic hearts in the centers.

Beidemann explained to George that he and Yousef were on their way to the plantation to get things ready. He promised him that when they got together again they would have a proper party.

A taxi responded to Beidemann's hand signal and pulled over to the curb. The shocks groaned on the old Citroen as the huge man lowered himself into the back seat. George waved good-bye to him and the still pale Yousef. The Moroccan said nothing, merely looked pathetic and gave a weak grin as the taxi pulled out into the throng of carts, trucks, cars, bicycles, and people from a dozen bloodlines and cultures.

Van answered George's knock on the door, letting in the bandy-legged Montagnard. George was a near perfect example of the rugged men of the hill tribes of Vietnam. A little taller and stockier than most Vietnamese, his teeth had been filed down during puberty rites. Those in the front were the ones that had been replaced with gleaming gold caps. He had fought with Van and Casey in Vietnam, and before that during the days of the Viet Minh and the French. He hated all communists no matter what their nationality. To him they were all either Cong or Viet Minh.

The old friends greeted each other. Casey felt a swelling of emotion at the sight of the tough little warrior, all one hundred and thirty pounds of him. George smiled, showing his oral gold mine. To foreigners, it seemed strange that gold teeth should have inlaid decorations such as hearts or diamonds of colored plastic, but it was a common practice in parts of Southeast Asia.

George and Van wasted no time. Looking at Casey, Van said quietly but with deep feeling, "It is time we visit Ling K'ai and pay our bill. It has been too long." Casey knew he was right. Only the honorable Ling K'ai— pimp, dope dealer, and smuggler—had known of their mission into Cambodia. It was he who had contacted the Kamserai rebels who aided them in their mission. K'ai was the only one who had a big enough ax to grind, and now it was time to balance accounts. He had been warned not to interfere, so what happened was now on his head. Casey had wanted to go with them to settle with Ling K'ai, but when they were on the run and holed up in the old temple in the swamp, he had given K'ai to George and Van. A deal was a deal.

From one of the rear bedrooms Van brought out a U.S. Army duffel bag. From the canvas sack he withdrew a custom-built, ten-round, twelve-gauge automatic shotgun. The barrel was sawed off to fourteen inches, with a collapsible wire stock and pistol grip. This was for George. Van selected his own favorite, a 9mm Walther P-38. Each man checked the clips, put extra ones in his pockets, and stood ready. They looked long and hard at Casey, knowing he wanted to go with them. They went silently to the door, moving as if they were embarrassed at not taking him with them. But they knew it would be best for him to remain behind while they took care of business their way. Singapore was not a place for Caucasians to be involved in murder.

Casey had a strange sense of being very much alone

when they had gone. He knew that for some months after
they'd returned from Cambodia, Ling K'ai had had men
watching them. He didn't know if that was still the case,
but in any event, there was little hope that George and
Van would catch him by surprise. *Goddammit!* he thought.
*Why the hell did I agree to this thing? They'll probably
walk right into a trap!*

Van and George walked out into the brilliant daylight,
taking their time. They were in no rush. Each savored
the day in his own way, each preparing himself for the
confrontation that had been so long delayed. From Sou
Phoung, the Kamserai chieftain, they had found out the
truth of what they had already suspected. On their behalf,
Sou Phoung had questioned a half-caste Portogee-Chinese
who worked for Ling K'ai. The Portogee had, on K'ai's
orders, informed the Khmer Rouge of their mission, and
was responsible for the deaths of several Kamserai men
and Yu Li's father.

Sou Phoung paid part of the debt by staking out the
half-caste over a bed of freshly cut, green bamboo and
leaving him there. In the tropics bamboo thrives and can
grow a foot or more a day. By the third day the half-
caste was raised six inches off the ground with several
long green shoots of bamboo extending from his chest
and abdomen. The half-caste's screaming had stopped
sometime during the second night, when one of the shoots
of thrusting bamboo inserted itself into his lungs. He'd
drowned in his own blood. At least it had ended the
unbearable agony of the green blades of death pushing
their way through his stomach and intestines.

Sou Phoung played the game the way the jungle demanded it be played. Compassion for an enemy was an

unknown commodity, completely alien to his thought processes.

George understood him perfectly, Van less so but with perhaps more sophistication. His hatred was on a more intellectual level and because of that, perhaps even more deadly.

The Golden Lotus Club sat on piles over the brown, murky waters of the basin in front of them. It was Ling K'ai's restaurant, and the headquarters of his drug and prostitution ring. It was here that Casey had killed K'ai's number one boy earlier in the year. Today they would kill the master, not the dog.

Entering through the front doors, Van and George made their way into the dark, silent interior, stopping for a moment to give their eyes a chance to adjust from the glare outside. Only the bartender was visible as he cleaned the bar and made preparations for the evening crowd. The Golden Lotus Club was open only for dinner and the late night trade. They headed for the rear of the restaurant where K'ai's office was, the sound of their heels loud on the polished tiles.

Out of the shadows, just in front of the office door, a new presence made itself known. "What is it you wish here?" The voice was soft, almost feminine. "What do you want here?" it asked once more.

Van spoke his answer nearly as softly. "We come for your master. Go away and don't involve yourself in that which is none of your concern."

The voice laughed quietly, easily, and the figure made itself visible. A pleasant-looking young man in loose, black peasant clothes bowed to them. "I am Sung Il Kim."

The light from an open doorway behind them showed

the smiling face of a well-built man, one supremely con-
fident of himself. "I know who you are, Van Tran Tich,
and you I have also heard of, savage," he said, speaking
to George. "We have been watching you. I knew when
you left your rooms. Know this: In me you see your
deaths." The words were spoken without bravado, almost
absentmindedly. "Are you prepared for your deaths?"
Not waiting for an answer, Kim motioned to a couple of
vague forms concealed in the shadows. Only their pistols
were visible, pointing at the two intruders. Kim walked
forward a step closer. "Drop your weapons or die now,"
he ordered. Van and George did as Kim instructed, the
pistol and shotgun clattering to the tile floor.

Kim stepped in front of them and bowed, straightening
himself into the *ap chak ay* preparatory position. Obviously enjoying himself, the young man made several
leaping passes and fake strikes at his stationary targets,
his movements proclaiming him a master of Tae Kwan
Do, the Korean style of the martial arts. When he finished
his demonstration, he stood still in front of his victims
while the men with the guns watched silently.

Holding his hands clenched, the knuckles touching at
the center of his solar plexus, he bowed once more,
saying, "It is time for you to die." Drawing into his
abdomen a long, deep breath, he began a rasping ex-
halation, pumping adrenaline into his system. Kim prepared to strike.

Before he could move, he hit the ground with a scream.
At what seemed to be the same instant, a double echo
reverberated through the club. Both of Kim's kneecaps
were shattered, and his legs bent back under him at impossible angles.

The two figures in the shadows detached themselves

from the darkness. One stepped forward. *"Ach! Meinen Freunden."* A wisp of smoke came from the action of Beidemann's Mauser HSc .380 automatic.

"Ali and I couldn't find the pilot we were supposed to find, and we got back to the hotel just as you were leaving. I saw men watching you, so we talked to Casey, found out where you were going, and got here in time to take care of the two men the young karate expert thought would be backing him up. Right now they are practicing to see how long they can hold their breath underwater. By now I believe they have set a new world record. They have been down at least fifteen minutes."

Sung Il Kim continued to moan in pain and shock, realizing what had happened all too clearly.

George walked over to the Korean. Bending over, he said softly, "Foolish one. Do you not know that everyone does not play the game by the same rules? If the big-nosed one here had not stopped you, we would have." George showed him the Colt .32 automatic he had hidden in a sleeve holster.

The young Korean looked up with pleading eyes. George stepped over him and picked up his shotgun as Van retrieved his P-38. The two Asians entered Ling K'ai's office, closing the door behind them.

Beidemann turned to Yousef. "Might as well get rid of this one too, yes? It is not wise to leave enemies behind when you can avoid it," he said, giving a nod to Yousef. The Moroccan slit the Korean's throat, then dragged the body back to the kitchen and tossed it out the rear door, where it sank into the filthy waters to join the two others already in residence.

Inside, Van and George were taking care of business with Ling K'ai, who had just awakened from an opium-induced sleep. That was why the shots outside had not disturbed his dreams. Neither had he been warned of the coming of Van and George. Kim had not wished to disturb him over something that could be dealt with so easily.

George grabbed the young Thai girl lying beside K'ai and threw her out the door, then closed and locked it. There would be no further interruptions. Van stood over K'ai and smiled, his soft, almost girlish features looking entirely too gentle for what was about to take place. George pulled his knife from its sheath at the base of his spine and stepped forward, humming softly to himself.

Outside, the big German and Yousef heard a hideous scream begin and last for what seemed an impossible length of time. It repeated itself over and over, each time becoming a little shorter in duration as if beginning to run down like a broken toy.

The door finally opened, and George and Van came out. Beidemann got one quick look at what remained of Ling K'ai, his head pinned to his mahogany desk by some shining object. After Van and George had performed some minor and some not-so-minor surgery, George had found a rifle-cleaning rod in K'ai's office, and in exchange for what K'ai had put into the ears of the Khmer Rouge, they had hammered the rod through his own ears and into his desk. The amount of time K'ai would continue to live was left entirely up to him. George had left his knife where K'ai could reach it. When the pain was too great, all the man had to do was cut his own throat with the one hand they had left him.

They had not yet reached the street outside the club when K'ai screamed again, took the knife, and with a trembling hand forced the blade into his neck. Twisting and ripping in his pain, he botched the job and had to hack at his own throat clumsily until at last he reached the jugular vein and bled to death.

George went back for a look, then returned to his friends and said simply, "It is best that it is over for him. He would never have been much good for a woman again anyway."

The debt had been paid. Now they were free to concentrate on their new contract across the sea in Africa.

They rejoined Casey, no one saying anything about the day's activities. Casey packed his belongings, and they all left together to find the Englishman. Before nightfall, they were in his plane and on their way to Malaya, where Harrison did a quick turn-around after letting his strangely silent passengers off at the private hangars. They loaded the Land-Rover for the ride from the hot, humid lands by the muddy river to the cooler heights of the mountains. Before dawn, they were on the red clay road leading up to Casey's plantation. The altitude was beginning to make itself known by the cooling of the morning air. They were almost home.

CHAPTER FIVE

Yu Li was waiting for them when they drove into the circular driveway in front of the main house, a large, rambling, white structure that spoke of colonial times and a memory of things gone but not completely forgotten.

Beidemann was impressed by the subtle security that had manifested itself on their approach to the compound where Yu Li was waiting. His instincts told him that they were under observation from the moment they entered the boundaries of Casey's domain. Even in the half-light of dawn he could make out the shapes of armed men set at ambush sites near the road. As they drove on, he noticed several claymore mines set along the sides of the road leading up the mountain. Where there were claymores, there had to be someone to activate them or else they would have gone off when the Land-Rover passed them.

Yu Li was standing on the porch, wearing a turquoise cheongsam, her hair piled high on her head. She had breakfast waiting for them on the veranda, where they could eat in the cool morning air, surrounded by the bright reds and purples of bougainvillea and other tropical shrubs. After seeing to their needs and assigning rooms, she left with Casey to the comfort of their own rooms. She had some needs of her own to take care of.

It was nearly three in the afternoon before all the guests were awake and moving. Yu Li always made it a point to try and get to know those with whom her man was going to do business. His life, and in a way hers, depended on them.

She was friendly but slightly formal to the big German, as if unsure of him and somewhat intimidated by his size. She knew that he and her man went back a long way together. Just how far back, she wasn't sure. Beidemann had to be pushing sixty, though he looked to be in his mid-forties and was as strong as a Celebes ox. Several times, when he and Casey were alone, they would speak German. When anyone came near, they would switch to English, and Yu Li guessed they were discussing something else. She had the feeling that there were some things concerning her man that Beidemann would never mention to her or to anyone else.

Casey wanted her to like his oldest surviving friend. He was the last of his kind. When the two men were alone he had asked Beidemann not to mention his being in the German army. He gave no reason, but he knew it wasn't necessary. Beidemann would do as he was asked, even if he didn't understand the reasons. Casey had almost not called Beidemann in for this mission, but he'd had the feeling that if he didn't, he'd never see the monster alive again. He was nearly as fascinated by the big man as Beidemann was with him. The German had an almost timeless quality to him that was more of the spirit than of age. The only change that time had made in Beidemann, other than making him a bit grayer and adding a few more lines to his face, was that he'd become a bit more mellow and sometimes chose to play a more fatherly or sophisticated role. He had fine manners when he chose to use them, and his natural good spirits were infectious. It didn't take long before he had Yu Li sitting on his knee like a child. Uncle Gus told her stories she found impossible to believe, but they were related with just enough feeling for truth that she was never quite sure. Beidemann was like something out of a legend to her, and she never quite believed he was a real person.

Ali ben Yousef, on the other hand, was easier for her to understand; his attitudes were less Western. That, and his quiet manner, made him more like one of her own people than Beidemann could ever be.

After a dinner of roast wild boar served on fine Austrian porcelain Yu Li had bought in Hong Kong, Casey escorted Beidemann and Yousef around the house. Van had chosen to stay by himself for a time. As with many Asians, he often had a need for the company of his own soul more than that of men. He and George shared a bungalow where they had recreated a small corner of Vietnam for themselves to enjoy.

Later that afternoon, Beidemann was startled when

two small figures attacked Casey. Leaping out from a cluster of palmetto fronds, Casey's legs were quickly trapped in the arms of two children, a boy and girl. Picking them up, one under each arm, Casey held them where they could do the least damage. He gave each a shake and kissed them, then set them down and patted each one on the rump, sending them off to find Yu Li.

Noting Beidemann's expression, Casey explained a bit self-consciously, "That's Nuyen and Quang, brother and sister. They were the only children on a boat over-loaded with refugees from Vietnam. Their small wooden boat had been raked over by a Viet gunboat, killing the children's mother and father, who were friends of Van's family. In the parents' personal effects was a letter by which Van was contacted when the survivors reached Malaya and were taken into custody. Between the three of us—me, Yu Li, and Van—we took care of the nec-essary paperwork, saw that squeeze was paid to the right people and that the kids were given to us. They were too young to know their birthdays, so we gave them the same one—the day Yu Li brought them here to the mountain." Beidemann noticed something in Casey's eyes that he had never seen before, a strange look of . . . was it guilt? Sadness? He couldn't tell which.

Clearing his throat, Beidemann changed the subject. "When do I meet the rest of your guests?"

Casey pointed to a trail leading off from the main compound, indicating that was the way Beidemann was to go. "Right now. They're all waiting for you, and I think you're going to have to prove to them that you're all that I said you were. So, old friend, be prepared."

At the phrase "old friend," Beidemann looked at his host and former tank commander. When Casey had gone by the name of Carl Langers from '43 to '45, he had looked to be the same age as Beidemann was then. The German would swear that he didn't look a year older now. Was it possible that he even looked a bit better? Maybe he'd had a face-lift. They could do wonderful things with silicone these days. . . . One day he was going to sit down and have a straight talk with *his* "old friend."

Beidemann followed Casey down the trail between giant trees draped with flowering vines. The green of the Cameron Highlands was incredible. The sun reflected off the leaves and branches of a thousand species of plants, casting an emerald glow over everything that moved inside the forest. Set in a separate clearing with its own cook shack was what served as the barracks for Casey's other guests. A long, narrow structure made of native wood and raised several feet off the floor of the forest on thick piles, the barracks could house over fifty men. At the edge of the clearing they were greeted by two sentries in camouflage fatigues, each armed with Spanish-made versions of the German G-3 rifle. Their salute to Casey was formal, if not rigid. They were not put on the job because they knew how to salute. They had been brought in because they knew how to fight and were dependable when it counted most.

Casey went up the steps to the barracks, then opened the screen door. As he stepped inside, those waiting for him were called to attention by a former sergeant major in Her Majesty's South African Rifles.

Jeremy Fitzhugh had been an eighteen-year-old private in World War II, and had served with distinction in North Africa, Sicily, and France. He'd retired from the regular army after twenty years and since then had sold his considerable talents to those whom he felt merited them the most. He was a professional mercenary, but he was a bit picky about whom he worked for.

"Ten-hut!" Twenty men halted whatever they were doing and jumped to attention beside their bunks.

"At ease," Casey said, walking with Beidemann between the rows of bunks, letting his friend get a good look at the men. The German knew several of them from other operations. Most were British, but there were a couple of Germans, South Africans, and Belgians tossed in for good measure. All had seen more than their share of action, and each had spent some time in Africa. Casey wanted men who knew the territory.

When they reached Fitzhugh they stopped and Casey made a formal introduction. "Sergeant Major Fitzhugh, may I present Gustaf Beidemann. He will be my second in command."

Beidemann stood nearly half a foot taller than Fitzhugh, but other than that, there was little difference in body design. Both were powerfully built men who knew their strength and would use it without reservation if called upon.

Beidemann and Fitzhugh eyed one another, each sizing up the other. At one time they had been enemies. Each needed to see if they were still going to be that way. There was a moment of tension as their eyes locked. Then the spell was broken. Beidemann was accepted when Fitzhugh came to attention, stamping his right foot down in the British fashion and, as he did so, barking out, "Sir! Regimental Sergeant Major Fitzhugh at your service!" There would be no trouble from Fitzhugh now. Once he'd recognized Beidemann as being his superior officer, he would do his part in all that was required of him.

Beidemann spoke to him easily. "I have heard of you, Sergeant. We have not always been on the same side, yet who can read the future? For now, let us keep the past where it belongs."

Casey picked up on that and spoke loud enough for everyone to hear. "That goes for everyone. We have a job to do, and I will not tolerate anything that could jeopardize our mission. If you have personal problems, leave them behind until you are finished with your contract. Understand this! Beginning at reveille tomorrow morning, anyone who does anything that threatens our security will be shot. There will be no other punishments, only death! There are too few of us to fight among ourselves, and in a very short time we will have all the trouble we need to keep ourselves entertained.

"Fitzhugh, you shall continue as senior noncom. From now on, please see that the men use the chain of command if they have any problems."

"Sir!" came Fitzhugh's response. He liked Casey's attitude.

Turning to Beidemann, Casey said, "They're all yours. Get them ready. We may have to leave sooner than planned. You and Fitzhugh work out who is going to be in each team, then bring me the list for final approval."

He left Beidemann to establish his authority in his own way. He had given the men until morning to get the shit out of their systems. He knew that his old friend would have to prove himself to the rest of the mercenaries before he would be completely in command.

Before the day was out, Beidemann had secured his leadership by putting two dissidents out of action for a couple of days. He was careful not to break anything, but he hurt them just enough to let them know who was

boss. It would be the last time anyone referred to his age
in anything but a respectful tone.

Casey invited those he considered his staff to dine at
the big house. After an evening meal of roast young
water buffalo, he, Van, Beidemann, and Fitzhugh went
into his study to discuss the mission. Neither Yousef nor
George was of much use for any deep thinking, and they
preferred to fix their own meals anyway. The two of
them had taken to each other, and Yousef had moved
into the bungalow with George and Van.

The others spent several hours going over maps supplied by van Janich. Using a magnifying glass, they went
over aerial shots of Dzhombe's palace and grounds. Casey
told them to take their time before making any comments.
He wanted each to get a feel of where they were going.

Beidemann studied the photos of the palace again and
again. At last, setting the glass down, he and Fitzhugh
looked at each other. Both knew what the other was
thinking. "I think we may have a problem," the German
said, pointing to the photos. "The drop zone is very
narrow, and many of our men have not had any recent
parachuting experience. If there are any crosswinds at
all, some of them are going to land outside the garden
walls, and if that happens, we will probably get our asses
blown away." Fitzhugh and Van nodded their agreement
to Beidemann's assessment of the situation. This was
another change that had come over Beidemann in the last
ten years. In the past he had always been a good soldier
but had preferred to leave the thinking to others. Casey
was glad to see his friend using his brain as well as his
brawn for a change.

He looked at the photos again, nodding his own agreement. "You're right. If there's over a ten-knot cross-

wind, we'll lose at least part of our men, and we don't have any to spare. Every man will be needed inside those walls if we're going to do the job. I don't know what the prevailing winds will be when we go in, but I'll find out. Let's plan for the worst; that way we won't be disappointed. How can we be certain of getting everyone in, especially the heavy weapons section? They're critical to the plan."

There was a long silence as each tried to come up with some kind of solution to the problem. Fitzhugh spoke first.

"Sir, I hate to give the bloody Huns any credit"—he smiled at Beidemann—"but they did do one thing that we might be able to copy. I was in Sicily when this happened, but didn't Otto Skorzeny, the SS commando, use gliders when he rescued Mussolini off that bloody great mountain? I don't remember the name of the place, but he didn't have much room to set down in."

Beidemann supplied the name. "It was the Gran Sasso d'Italia, and you're right. The winds were too bad to make a jump, and he used gliders to get his men in. Does anyone know how much ground a glider needs to set down in?"

Casey looked at the photos again. "I think they can put down in a couple of hundred feet. Look here." They gathered around one photo. "This shows what appears to be a large pond about seventy-five or a hundred feet long running toward the palace. At the end of the pond is another hundred feet of garden with trees on either side. If it's not too deep, a glider could probably touch down in it and slide up into the gardens without cracking up in the trees."

Van bobbed his head up and down. "I like it. But

where do we get a glider and a pilot?"

Casey grinned, his gray-blue eyes sparkling as he went to get a bottle of Jack Daniel's. "I don't know about the glider, but the pilot is going to be Harrison. Van, get on the radio. You'll probably find the limey—" He looked at Fitzhugh. "No offense meant."

"There is none, seeing as I am of Irish descent," Fitzhugh responded a bit testily.

Casey bowed his head, accepting the minor rebuke. "As I was saying, you'll probably find him at Mama Chin's in Kuala Lumpur. Call the airfield and have someone there tell him to get his tail up here as soon as possible."

Van left to make the call as Casey said to Beidemann, "Harrison told me once that he got started by flying gliders when he was a kid. Soaring, he called it. Hell, that bastard soars half the time even when he hasn't left the ground, but he's the best pilot in this neck of the woods and can fly anything with wings or rotors up to and including commercial jets. Gus, you don't really know him, but Fitzhugh and Van can vouch for him. He was with the SAS, the British Special Air Service, for five years. That's their equivalent of the American Green Berets, so you can believe he's good. Besides which, he'll do damn near anything for a profit. I don't know what he does with his money, but in five years I've never seen him buy a drink for anyone or spend a cent he didn't have to."

Van came back at the end of Casey's description and said, "Oh, you're still talking about Harrison. Well, old warthog," Van said in a cockney accent he had picked up in London when his father had served with the South Vietnamese Foreign Service there, "our dashing young pilot will be here in the morn for kippers and scones. I told him you had something which could buy him an earldom when he returned to jolly old England."

"Good! Now see that a cable is sent to Major Shan in Taipei. Tell him to get over here. We'll have him put his machinery to work and find us a glider large enough to carry the heavy weapons section and Gus's crew. We'll make the jump with only those who have the most parachuting experience. The rest will go on the glider, if we can find one."

Van left to call in the cable to Major Shan, asking him to come and visit with his old friends, and maybe do a little hunting.

CHAPTER SIX

The next day, Harrison, in a near coma, was delivered with his kit bag to the plantation by a Malay cab driver who demanded extra payment from Casey for the abuse his old Morris taxi had suffered getting up the mountain. Casey had seen Harrison on one of his occasional benders before. There was nothing to do but find a corner to put him in until he sobered up, and that could take a couple of days. He'd be awake tomorrow but in no condition to communicate. Harrison looked like an alcoholic version of a thirtyish David Niven, right down to the out-of-style, pencil-line mustache. Lean, slightly paranoid after having dealt with Casey and his crew before, Har-

rison was almost a member of the family. His condition
didn't bother Casey, who wouldn't need him for a while
yet, not until he'd spoken with Major Shan, who'd confirmed that he would arrive on Tuesday, two days hence.

Even though they had to wait, that was no reason not
to start their mission training. Beidemann took charge,
Fitzhugh enforcing his orders with proper British bellowing and cursing. Up and down the sides of the mountain they ran, loaded down with field packs filled with
wet sand. Beidemann knew that legs were a soldier's
lifeline. If the legs went, then so did everything else. He
also dispelled any further illusions about his age being
a handicap. He and Fitzhugh ran the other mercs' asses
into the ground.

Beidemann would often take the lead, ordering them
to follow him. Breaking off the trails and heading cross
country, not bothering to look for breaks in the brush
and vines, he just charged through, dragging the others
in his wake. In less than a day he had at least half the
mercs believing he was some kind of jungle superman
who would have been more at home in the trees than on
the ground. Casey took his training with them and cursed
his old pal for being in such disgustingly good shape.
Only George seemed to have no problem keeping up
with the monster, and he saw to it that Yousef didn't lag
too far behind.

In the two days that passed before Major Shan showed
up, Beidemann had the mercs doing everything but goose-
stepping through the jungle, and he promised them they'd
do that sometime the following week.

Part of their day was spent building a mock-up of the
palace and its grounds, using a clearing a couple of miles
from the house. Until they left for the mission they would
spend most of their time there, going over every step of

their assignment, rehearsing until they knew the layout of the palace and grounds better than Dzhombe's staff did. If Beidemann could have had his way, they would have rehearsed the job blindfolded.

Each of the men had his specialty: demolitions, commo, medic, light and heavy weapons. Besides their individual talents, they were all veterans of jungle warfare and raider-style operations. They'd do!

Their plan for getting out of Kimshaka didn't call for them to spend any time in the bush, but Casey insisted that they always plan for the worst. George gave them a couple of classes in jungle survival and a short demonstration of the use of the machete as a weapon. He could split a man from crown to navel in one swipe.

Major Shan was delivered to the plantation by the same Malay cabby who had brought Harrison. He tried to get Casey to go for a monthly rate but had no luck.

Shan was in mufti, impeccably attired in the best that Taipei's tailors had to offer: a light blue sharkskin suit, white patent leather Guccis, and a London Fog trench coat. A bit taller than the average Chinese, his hair had just enough gray in it to give him a distinguished look, which he cultivated.

Yu Li greeted him in the old style as matron of the house. She bowed him inside and left him alone after setting out a tray of rice cookies. Casey had to come up from the training area. He was tired and sweaty, and in no mood to waste time. He started to send for Harrison but decided against it. He'd let him in on things later. Harrison hadn't even asked why he was there. He was content just to be breathing. Casey felt one more day of rest would do him good. There was no reason to upset him at this point.

Wasting no time, Casey got to the heart of the matter.

"Glider, Major—I want a glider. One large enough to carry fifteen men and their gear, including two sixty-millimeter mortars, a fifty-seven millimeter recoilless rifle, and ammo for the works. If we can't get a glider, the timetable may have to be put off until we can figure out something else."

Having already spent a large portion of his advance money for arranging the contract, Shan protested vigorously at any delay. "You must be on time," he demanded. "You have a contract. What is this thing about gliders? No one has used gliders since World War Two."

Casey was adamant. "Find me a glider, you son of a bitch, or jump into the damned place yourself. I have Harrison up here, and as soon as he's finished drying out, I expect you to have found me one. While you're at it, you'd better get two or three in case he cracks up during practice."

Shan raged in frustration. "Now you want *three* of them? What do you think I am?"

Casey scowled at him. "I know what you are and so do you. So cut the crap and get me what I need, or the people in Africa are going to be very upset with you."

They argued for some time before Shan relented. "I will do my best. That's all I can promise." That was good enough. Casey wasn't terribly fond of Shan, but the man could get things done when he wanted to. If there were gliders to be had, he would get them. He didn't tell Shan that he would go on the mission anyway, even if they all had to jump in.

Major Shan again wondered why Casey Romain always seemed to get him off-balance when he, a senior officer in Taiwan's Ministry of Security, was obviously a much more intelligent and cultured person.

He sighed deeply. *The world is full of these long-nosed cretins,* he thought. Where had the graceful life gone? *If it had not been for that incredibly bad run of luck at the gambling tables in Macao, I would not have to degrade myself by doing business with these degenerates.* The honorable major grumbled to himself all the way back down the mountain, not stopping until the cab reached the airfield at Kuala Lumpur.

Harrison came in shortly after Shan left, his David Niven looks more serene now that most of the whiskey was gone from his system. His hands had stopped trembling to the point where he could hold a cup of coffee. His voice was still a bit husky, sounding a shade like Sydney Greenstreet in the movie *Casablanca*. He was dressed in tailored khakis with a green and white polka dot ascot. He used his swagger stick of polished ebony to whisk away a bothersome fly from his face. Clearing his throat, he rasped, "Where's the bar?" Spying it in the corner of the living room, he started for it but was intercepted. Casey got between him and the object he wanted most: a bottle of Hennessy just out of reach behind the back of the square-built master of the house.

Before Casey would let him have even a smell of the cognac, he forced Harrison to listen to his proposal. There was a period of negative response from the pilot before Casey reached the right numbers. Harrison poured a tumbler to the brim and drained the amber fluid as if it were a glass of water in the middle of a desert.

"I don't believe you've talked me into this thing, but I am too weak to argue. You know, old chap, that I desperately try to avoid anything that remotely resembles violence. Why do you constantly play on my sense of greed to get me to do these outrageous things for you?"

Harrison affected his most indignant posture from his repertoire of wounded looks and attitudes while he poured himself another cognac. "Really, Casey, it is damned unfair of you to take advantage of my weaknesses. One of these days you're going to get me hurt."

Casey smiled as he took the bottle away from the man. The image of Harrison speaking as if he were a delicate flower was amusing. One did not survive years with the SAS if one was less than the best, and the swagger stick Harrison carried was for more than just appearance. Harrison had long ago mastered kendo and Philippine stick fighting. He was always full of indignant protests, but in his own mind he was the last of England's great gentlemen adventurers and knights errant, looking for his own Holy Grail to pursue.

No, thought Casey, *it would not do to underestimate this Englishman.* Harrison was usually referred to as "the limey," but only by his friends. Anyone else who took such a liberty did so at his own risk. Harrison tried to persuade Casey to give him one more touch of the precious liquid, but now that a deal had been made he accepted, as graciously as he could, Casey's refusal on the grounds that from now on Harrison was under orders and in training. The pilot would have probably made a stronger protest, but Casey reminded him that once the glider was on the palace grounds, so was he. He'd have to take his chances with the rest of them.

Due to his special status as a pilot, he was quartered at the big house. It also made it easier to see that he didn't fall victim to temptation and hit the bottle during a moment of soul-searching.

Beidemann and Fitzhugh kept the pressure on. Between the two of them, they ran everyone's ass, including

Casey's, ragged. While Shan searched for gliders, they trained nonstop. *Run to the firing range! Run to the barracks! Run to where the running and exercise area was located!* Some of the men grumbled at what they considered an excessively demanding training regimen, but the complaints soon disappeared when Fitzhugh reminded them that they were going to be the only pale faces in a black crowd, and if anything went wrong, they'd need their legs to get the hell out, and God help the slow ones. The next day they set a record for their daily five-mile run. Fear is a great motivator, and the smart man will use it to spur himself and others to greater efforts.

Run and fire. Down, up, hit the ground. Dig in, up, run, roll. Fire team exercises, one covering the other while they leapfrogged forward. Fighting withdrawal exercises usually ended the day's activities, since that was how they would have to get out of the palace and the city.

Each man was ordered to memorize the complete layout of the palace at Kimshaka and its grounds. The routes into and out of the city had to be known by everyone. Constant rehearsal at their mock-up, where the palace buildings were represented by logs, made certain that every man would know where he was at any given moment. Alternate planning also came into play. It was always necessary to plan for the worst, to know what to do if the job went down bad.

It was ten days before Shan reached Casey, who was in Kuala Lumpur with Harrison picking up supplies. Shan ran him down at Mama Chin's, where he usually ate when in town. Mama, a huge Tonkinese woman with a single long braid, a full set of gold teeth, and an endless smile, called Casey to the phone in the kitchen.

"Mr. Romain, I have found your gliders. It was most difficult, but I have them in Taiwan. One is still in its crate awaiting assembly, but the other is ready for use." Casey had to get Mama to quiet the kitchen help, then had Shan repeat the information.

Covering the mouthpiece of the phone, he told Harrison, "He's found your birds."

Harrison nudged him. "Ask what kind they are."

Removing his hand from the mouthpiece, he said, "Major Shan, Harrison wants to know what kind they are."

Shan chuckled over the phone. "I believe they are what was known as American Wacos when they were used by the Chindits during the Burma campaign." Harrison was close enough to the phone to hear Shan's reply.

"Did he say Chindits? Wacos? Burma?" he cried. "You mean those bloody things are leftovers from World War Two? My God, they must be nearly as old as Gus!" Casey decided not to tell Beidemann what Harrison had said. His tall friend was getting a bit touchier lately. He pushed Harrison away from the phone and told him to shut up.

"Major Shan, where are you calling from?"

"Not a mile away from you. I am at the Kuala Lumpur Imperial by the park. Now listen to me! The glider in the crate is already on its way to your staging area; the other is in Taiwan. I heard your Englishman's response. As long as he is with you, you might as well send him over to me, and we will return to Taiwan on my private plane. It would be best if he practiced where I could have some control over the security."

Casey grunted in agreement. "All right, Shan, but

why the hell do you sound so pleased today?"

Shan chuckled again. "Two reasons, my homely associate. First, a nice profit was made on the gliders. Second, I may be able to watch one of your degenerate friends commit hara-kiri in the antique I have for him to practice on. Really, it is the kind of thing I have long dreamed of. I only wish that you were the pilot instead of Harrison. Now send him over to me today, and we will get on with what has to be done. You still have a time schedule to meet. Good-bye, Mr. Romain."

Harrison continued to moan as he got into the cab to go over to the Kuala Lumpur Imperial.

"Casey, old boy, my dear friend, I really do think we should reconsider my participation in this venture."

Casey promised to send the rest of his kit to Taiwan in a couple of days.

CHAPTER SEVEN

Harrison joined Major Shan at his hotel, where he was given no time to do anything but get into a waiting cab to be driven to the airport. Shan's DC-3 was waiting with the engines running. Much to Shan's amusement, the Englishman questioned him nonstop about the condition of the gliders. Harrison didn't pause even when the DC-3 reached altitude and headed east over the Cameron Highlands, passing over Temerloh in the mountains, then over Kuantan on the east coast before entering the air space of the South China Sea. From there, the pilot took a heading that would keep Sarawak and Sabah to starboard. They made one stop for fuel at Baguio in the

Philippines, then continued on to Tainan Air Force Base on Taiwan.

When the old DC-3 touched down on the tarmac, she rolled up to a tin hangar and stopped. Shan took Harrison by closed car to the same building where Casey Romain and his men had stayed before going on the Cambodian contract the previous year. He left Harrison alone for a time and returned to his office to check on the arrangements for the transport of Casey's unit to the staging area. Not even Shan knew exactly where they were going, or when the hit would be made, and he really didn't care. Once word was received that Matthew Dzhombe was dead, he would receive the balance of his commission for setting up Casey with the white Africans.

Much to Shan's irritation, Harrison spent the next three days getting the old Waco reskinned with new canvas, but the pilot had refused to go up in the thing until new canvas had been laid on. The original was so rotten it could be torn apart by a child's hands.

Shan had done well on the glider deal. He had located them in a warehouse at a small airfield near Pingtung. They were indeed leftovers from World War II and had been forgotten when no one had any further need of them. He'd bought them from the field commander for three hundred American dollars and had sold them to the contractors for five thousand each. Not a bad day's work.

Once the glider was in good enough condition that Harrison was willing to make a test flight, Shan showed him a chart of the area near the town of Chingpu on the east coast. There was a clearing there with dimensions almost identical to the one on which Harrison would have to set down at Dzhombe's palace. Harrison knew he couldn't stall any longer; the glider was as good as it was ever going to be. He told Shan.

"Okay, let's set up a run," Shan said.

Using Shan's own DC-3 for a tow plane, Harrison had the Waco loaded with sandbags equal to the weight that would actually be on board. Harrison strapped himself into the pilot's seat, said a Hail Mary even though he was Church of England, and released the brake. The DC-3 taxied down the runway and lifted off. He was surprised at how smooth the takeoff was. Trailing behind the silver, twin-engine plane by a rope umbilical cord, Harrison and his Waco were taken over a ridge of mountains rising to over three thousand feet. The flight to the landing zone would take less than three quarters of an hour.

Once over Chingpu, he had the pilot of the DC-3 go around four times while he checked out the field below. Finally he couldn't stand the tension anymore and released the cable. He was free and on his own.

Three days later, a forlorn and tattered-looking Harrison showed up at the plantation. He'd come back without Shan. Casey had to hold back a laugh as Harrison entered the living room, his head covered with bandages. He had a definite limp, but it was obvious he wasn't seriously hurt.

Beidemann came in right behind him. "Well, Englishman, how did it go?"

Harrison pulled himself erect and snapped, "I do not have to take any crap from you, you great bleedin' rotter. Remember, *we* won the war, not you."

Beidemann was a little shocked by the hostility in Harrison's response and said, "That's only because I spent most of my time on the Eastern Front. You tell him, Cas—" He was stopped by a sharp move of Casey's hand, which told him to knock it off and change the subject. He did. Going to Harrison, he put his arms around him and picked him up. It looked as if a normal-size man were trying to comfort a child. Ignoring Harrison's protests, he kissed the Englishman wetly on both cheeks. "Not to worry. Uncle Gus will take care of you." Casey told him to put Harrison down, which he did, dropping him to the floor and further denting the pilot's dignity.

After Harrison was back on his feet, Casey handed him a cognac and asked, "How was it?"

Harrison sat down heavily on a leather sofa before answering. "I can do it, but only once more and then I never want to speak to you again. The only reason I am going through with it is because Shan said the plane in the other crate had good canvas and termites hadn't eaten away the wing support struts. When that godforsaken antique finally stopped, it threw me clear through the bloody windshield! That's why I'm all cut up."

"What about your seat belt?" Casey inquired.

"Seat belt?" shrieked Harrison. "The reason I'm walking around like the bleedin' hunchback of Notre Dame is because the goddamned seat belt was the only thing in the entire plane that wasn't rotted clear through! The bloody seat belt held me to the bloody seat, which ripped and followed me through the bloody windshield!" Harrison leaned back, exhausted, and gulped his drink in an attempt to drown the memory.

Casey turned to Beidemann, who had been joined by Van and Fitzhugh. "I think Harrison's a bit upset, gentlemen, but if I understand him, he says it's a go."

Harrison raised his eyes, trying to look more wounded

than he was. "That is correct. We leave in three days. The contractors, according to Shan, will pick us up in one of their aircraft and transport us to the staging area, wherever that is. The plane will have consular status and therefore will entitle us to a certain amount of diplomatic immunity. It won't be searched or inspected at any of the refueling stops along the way."

"Good enough," said Casey, turning to Beidemann and Van. "Get your men ready, and have them clean up any sign of them ever having been here. I want the area sterilized. Each man is to write instructions for the disposition of his share in the event he doesn't make it back. They're to give them to Yu Li by tomorrow evening at the latest. She'll see that they are followed to the letter, according to our agreements."

Pouring a round for everyone, Casey toasted them with the ancient salute of the Roman gladiators before they fought. Beidemann had seen him do this a number of times and still did not understand the strange look that always appeared in his friend's eyes when he made the old toast: *"Ave Caesar! Te moritu, te salutes.* Hail Caesar! We who are about to die salute you."

Graveyard humor was common enough among men like these, and no one thought the toast an ill omen or out of place. Each accepted the possibility of his own termination as an occupational hazard. They were ready for whatever fate was in store for them. Three days to Africa.

"By the way, Harrison, all your shots are up-to-date, aren't they?" queried Casey, who already knew the answer.

"Shots? What shots?" Harrison grew instantly leery. "You're not going to shoot me up with those awful bleedin' needles! No, sir! Not me! I've never caught anything, not even the ruddy clap!"

Casey tried to ease some of his mental anguish. "Yu Li will do it. She has a delicate touch." Taking Harrison's arm, he led him to a small room off the rear porch and turned him over to Yu Li, who smiled sweetly and removed several hypodermics from a glass medical case. To Harrison, most of them resembled ice picks more than they did instruments of healing.

Leaving him to Yu Li's tender ministrations, Casey returned to the living room. The others had left to take care of their men and prepare for the upcoming flight.

Yu Li joined him a few minutes later, looking pleased. He caught a brief glimpse of Harrison limping off to his room.

Casey and Yu Li spent most of the following three days with the children. He liked to watch them at play. There was something restful about them. He wished he could spend more time with them but knew that Yu Li more than made up for it. They spent more time than usual in each other's arms during those days. Even for one such as he, there was never any telling of what the future held.

Beidemann and Fitzhugh increased their efforts to make certain their men would be ready. As Casey had ordered, the area was sterilized. If any of them were killed or had to be left behind, there would be no way they could be traced to the plantation. Even the movements that had brought them to Malaya had been covered through the use of false passports and visas provided them, at Casey's request, by the contractors. Having a government sponsor on a mission certainly made such things easier.

Gear was packed and stored, weapons were returned

to the arms room and locked away, and letters were given to Yu Li, who hoped she would be able to return each of them to the writer but knew there was little chance of that.

Beidemann had even quit drinking. Much to his dismay, he found that he didn't have quite the resilience he used to boast about. Time does take its insidious toll.

Fitzhugh went about things as if it were just a training exercise. The others, including George, Van, and Yousef, looked forward to the coming operation. Men like them needed periodic injections of action to make their lives seem worthwhile.

Casey read constantly, trying to cram into his memory everything that could possibly be of value once they reached their destination. He studied photos of his target for hours, trying to see behind the shiny black face into the man's mind. Dzhombe was a lot of bad things, but he was still a hell of a man and wouldn't go down easily. Another name for a black face flashed into Casey's mind, one he hadn't thought of in many, many years. *Jubala*. There was a faint resemblance between the two men, and if it went to the limit, then, as with Jubala, he would kill Matthew Dzhombe.

At four in the morning of the third day, Casey and his men drove through the open end of the runway outside Kuala Lumpur to where a twin-engine jet waited. The pilot greeted them with obvious distaste. Casey didn't give a damn as long as he knew how to fly and took them where they were supposed to go. The early morning darkness had a heavy dampness to it, smelling strongly of the thousands of miles of jungle and ocean around the field.

The men were silent as they loaded their gear and

boarded the plane. Even though they were wearing civilian clothing, anyone who looked at them could have easily determined that they were anything but bored businessmen out on a junket. When they reached the staging area, they would have one week to adjust themselves to the new climate and have one last frantic burst of training before going into action.

The door closed behind them, cutting off the outside world. Engines started and turbines spun, revving up to 4,500 rpm before fuel was fed to them, then to 8,000 rpm before the brakes were released. The jet taxied to the end of the runway, turned around in a tight circle, and then the pilot gave it full throttle. They were up. The landing gear was raised. Before the sun rose they would be over the white beaches of the Andaman Islands.

The sleek jet flew on. Whispering through the dark sky, it seemed to be racing the sun. Beyond the Andamans they would make a stop at Colombo in Sri Lanka. From there they would fly across the Somali coast, head a bit south, then go on to Kenya for another refueling at Nairobi. Some of the mercs slept; others played cards or just sat with their thoughts. Most grew a bit restless during the long hours of idleness after the past weeks of hectic training.

From Nairobi it was another fifteen hundred miles before they touched down at the capital of the white contractors, Regisburg. The flight was timed so they would land at night. For the first time since departing Malaya, they were permitted to exit the aircraft, and then only to take the two dozen steps to where they boarded a propeller plane closely related to the American Caribou cargo and troop transport so popular in Vietnam, a plane that could take off from a rice paddy and land on a football field.

Not a word was spoken to them as they made the transfer, but they welcomed the brief chance to stretch their legs and smell the strange air of Africa. Most wished they could have had a few hours in the city, whose lights bounced off a low bank of clouds to the north. Lights were where one would find women and whiskey. But there was always later, when they had pockets full of money.

The cargo plane lurched forward, then thrust its blunt nose into the air, rising with its new and unfamiliar cargo of killers, then flying inland to where a dry lake bed would be its landing field. They flew across the borders of several nations, then crossed the lesser tributary of the Congo River known as the Lualaba. They skirted Lubumbashi, formerly Elisabethville, to avoid the airport's radar, then headed south.

The first burning rays of the sun reflected off the starboard side of the plane as she set down in a cloud of red dust whipped up by the whirling props as the blades were reversed. The men who were sleeping were jerked into instant awareness by the landing. They were down! They were here!

As the cargo master opened the door to the outside, Casey stood behind him and wondered if their target had any idea of what was coming for him.

CHAPTER EIGHT

Matthew Dzhombe, the Avenging Lion of Kimshaka, watched with pleasure the passing of his favorite regiment, the ufaSimba. As with the first Shaka, they were given the name meaning "haze" to signify the manner in which they surrounded their enemies and destroyed them. *Simba* meant lion in Swahili, and if strangers chose to call them lions, then that did not displease him either, for they were his lions.

Very few knew his great secret. Only his mother and the wizards of his home village had seen the signs at his birth that marked him as the inheritor of Shaka, first of the great Zulu kings. It was he who had brought the warring tribes of the southern Bantu under one standard.

The passing fighters of the ufaSimba saluted with Kalashnikov rifles. The loincloths, ostrich feathers, shields, and short spears of the original "Haze" warriors were now replaced by camouflage uniforms and automatic weapons. Behind them, rolling up dust on the streets, came several armored vehicles—American half-tracks and British Saladin armored cars—Dzhombe's only motorized infantry force. There were a few vintage Russian T-34 tanks in his army, but these were usually in need of maintenance and out of service. He was woefully short of diesel mechanics.

The ufaSimba made their turn, marching around the corner of the palace and out of sight. Dzhombe watched them with affection. They were the roots by which his tree of power would grow until all of southern Africa lay in the shade of its branches.

He had come far from his native kraal to be here at this moment, at the head of a nation named after his soul spirit, Shaka.

Before he had received his *umuTsha,* the slit-skin loincloth, at his puberty rites, his mother and the *um-Thakathi* of his clan had told him of his heritage. His mother was of the same bloodline as was Nandi, the Great Mother who had given birth to Shaka. It was she who had introduced him to the mysteries that were to guide the course of his life and told him of his favored place with the gods. This was all confirmed by the wizards who taught him the rituals and secrets that brought the gods to him in his sleep after he would drink of their magic potions made with secret herbs and plants. Then, in his dreams, he knew the truth. He was Shaka reborn, and as Shaka had done before him, he would rule as supreme master. After a few years he no longer needed the potions to bring the gods to him in his dreams, and now they came whenever he willed it, reassuring him of their favor—and of their punishment should he disobey them. They had even given him the body of Shaka, over six feet in height with the same massive arms and chest endowed with the strength of a Cape buffalo.

During his youth he had acquired all the known skills of his soulmate, becoming a master of the spear. And by the time he was fourteen, he had killed both leopard and lion by himself, hunting them alone to prove his worthiness of the mantle of power. On his body were the scars left by the claws of the leopard. It was the spirit of Shaka that gave him the strength to defeat the beast. Dzhombe remembered standing over the great cat's body, his spear above his head, bleeding from a dozen cuts as he cried out to the gods his thanks for their gift to him. In his child's play he even had a secret place named after the capital of the first Shaka, kwaBulawayo, "the place of he who kills."

It had taken time to bring his small tribe into a position of supremacy over their more numerous neighbors, time and death, the latter dealt out with a free hand. Soon he would be ready to move to reclaim the lands taken from his fathers, and he would make the whites pay for it. With the money they paid to use his railway line, he had made arrangements to buy sophisticated weaponry that would soon be brought to him from the armories of Europe. Then he would move south. No one would stand against him and live, white or black. Then, when he had done this, his *impis* would turn their faces to the north and begin the long march that would bring all of Africa under his rule, for such was the destiny of those born to be king.

He was relieved when the ceremonies were over. This

was to be his last official act before returning to his home kraal for the rites of rebirth and renewal. Only his most loyal officers knew where he would be. They were all men from his tribe whom he had raised to power. Their fate was tied to his. If he died or fell, so would they. He was the man who held all the strings of power in one hand, and they knew it.

Under the cover of darkness, Dzhombe left his palace taking with him only three men as an escort. He wore, as did they, the uniform of a private in the ufaSimba. Sitting in the back of the nondescript weapons carrier, a floppy bush hat cast his face even further into the shadows of the night. The men with him were all of his clan and his tribe. They would offer their bodies to protect him. In the secret places of their souls, they believed Dzhombe to be more than just mortal man.

Dzhombe reinforced that concept with brutal regularity. In the interrogation rooms of his palace, they had seen him kill strong men by crushing the life out of them with his bare hands as if his victims had been no more than sickly children. Several times he had dismembered those who angered him by ripping off their arms at the shoulders, and sometimes he would place one of his giant hands on the head of the unfortunate man and squeeze ever so slowly, gradually increasing the pressure of his fingers. Dzhombe took his time with his demonstrations of power so the impression he made on those who witnessed his actions would stay with them forever. They would remember everything they had seen and bear witness to those not present. Even the most hardened of Dzhombe's ufaSimba felt sympathy for the victim. As they watched, they seemed to feel the bones of their own skulls begin to give way, the unrelenting pressure of those huge fingers increasing until the victim's mouth opened involuntarily to howl like a wounded beast. His men's mouths would open spontaneously when the victim's did, as the pressure to the skull was transmitted to the jaw-bone. Blood would begin to flow from nostrils, ears, and scalp as the thick nails of Dzhombe's fingers tore through the flesh of the head to ultimately crush the doomed man's skull like an eggshell. And through it all, Dzhombe's face showed no sign of the tremendous power it took for his fingers to complete the grisly task.

There were other times when those chosen to be his personal guards were bound even closer to him by par-ticipating in ancient rituals after the executions, by shar-ing the flesh of Dzhombe's victims, by eating the heart, liver, and brains. Dzhombe had them swear great oaths to him that could never be broken. Like him, his men came from the kraals of the forests. None had been con-taminated by Western education. They were still the chil-dren of primal forces and faith. They would serve him as they were sworn to.

All that night they drove, leaving the warrens and hovels of Kimshaka City behind, returning to the clean, pure life of kraal and clan. There the air was touched only by the honest smoke of cooking fires and not the vile urban pollution of gasoline and diesel fumes.

At the entrance to the valley where his home kraal lay, the weapons carrier stopped. Waiting to greet him were the *umThakathi*, the wise men and good wizards of his tribe, and those who were to be the privileged participants in the rites of renewal. He would stand before them, and they would remove the trappings of the West from his body until he stood naked. Sacred oils and ash would be spread upon him to remove any contamination brought with him from the outside world. He had to be as in the beginning.

Bowing low before their master, the participants prostrated themselves, each falling to his face to crawl before him as he placed his foot on their heads. Then, rising to their knees, they would throw their heads back and offer him their knives, symbolizing total submission. Sometimes, just to make his point, Dzhombe would accept the proffered blade and slice the exposed throat. The others would make no comment. What he did was his right, for they were his to do with as he chose. They belonged to him body and soul. He could take what he wished. It was good.

The entrance to the valley would be guarded by his men. No one would be permitted to enter the valley or interrupt the ceremony. Until he left, anyone who came to the valley would be turned back or killed. Over the years the neighboring tribes had learned to keep their distance during these times.

In the deep bush near the escarpment, where the mountains dropped from the cloud-covered heights to the lush heaviness of the jungle, Matthew Dzhombe walked upon a trail used for uncounted centuries by those of his clan. Behind him came the others who were to celebrate this sacred ritual, fifteen warriors and three *umThakathi*. They followed in the wake of the huge, sweating body clad only in his *umuTsha*. Bearing packs that contained the things they would later require, they moved silently through the mist-shrouded trees. Like their leader, they too wore paint smeared in mystical whorls and circles upon their ash-coated bare bodies. Each had his hair plastered down under a thick cap of red river mud in which were implanted ostrich feathers and the brilliant plumage of the red and green bird who screamed like a woman in labor.

In the center of the line of men were three young girls of thirteen and fourteen, shoulders and budding breasts covered by drab, homespun cotton mantles. The *lobola*, the bride price, had been paid for each of them in full. Their parents were pleased and honored that their daughters had been chosen. The girls walked wearily, heads downcast. Their movements were those of ones who had reconciled themselves to an unknown fate. Their young age prevented them from fully appreciating the great honor being shown them, but they would obey. During the trek from their village they had not been abused or hurt. To the contrary, they were treated with great kindness and consideration by the naked warriors, and each girl was still a virgin.

Dzhombe looked to the sky. Through a break in the trees he could see the mountains where the gods of his fathers lived. It was to them he had been dedicated when he reached puberty and had gone through the initiation rites that entered him into manhood and the privileged membership of his clan. Every year since then he had participated in the rites. He knew that to fail in this would lead to disaster, for the gods would turn their faces from him, and his enemies would destroy him and his people. Here, where great waters fell from the lips of the gods to form the rivers that fed the lowlands, he and his warriors would once more make the earth fertile as had been done since the beginnings of memory. He regretted that no young men were of the right age to take their place in the rites, but ten years earlier a bad time of disease and drought had wiped out nearly all the young males who would now be the proper age. Next year there would be new blood added to the clan.

By the waterfalls known as the Breath of the Mountain, they made camp. Here they would fast for three days to purify the body and spirit. During that time the girls were permitted to do much as they pleased as long as they did not wander from the camp. The girls made for themselves a rude shelter of palm leaves tied to a frame of thin saplings. The mist from the waterfall never ceased. All day and all night it cast its eerie shroud over the men as they sat in a circle by a fire chanting and singing.

From their palm-leaf hut the girls watched the men with a mixture of fear and anticipation. They knew they were to be brides, but they did not know any of the details of their marriage ceremony. It was the unknown part that frightened them. It was truly an honor to be the bride of Dzhombe or one of his clan. But why was the ceremony to be held so far from their village where there would be no witnesses, as there had been for the other girls who had been given as brides to the young men?

At dawn on the fourth day of purification, the *um-Thakathi* cast dried leaves and herbs into the fire, and the men breathed deeply of the smoke. The herbs were liberally laced with *ganga* to heighten the senses, to put them on a higher plane where the grass beneath their feet felt as soft as the young breasts of the brides-to-be. When thorns were pressed against their bare flesh, it felt as if warm lips were caressing their bodies. It was time. . . .

The three girls were brought forth. The wizards shaved their heads and covered their bodies with a paste of animal fat and ash. Then they were made to breathe the smoke of the fire until their eyes grew glazed and red, tears running down their cheeks as they leaned over the coals to breathe deeply. Fear left them as their minds floated on the smoke. Around them the men formed a circle and chanted. The girls began to dance. Stepping up to the fire, then turning to face the circle of men, they moved back and forth to a timeless rhythm. They had never danced this way before nor did the wizards tell them what they were to do. Somehow they just knew what was to be done. Eyes glazed, bodies trembling, both men and brides knew the time was near. Anticipation of the completion of the marriage act made the area between their young thighs moist and the men erect.

Dzhombe lay on his back, naked. Each of the maidens was brought to him by the men, then held over his body and lowered on him until the hymen broke. When each had been penetrated, they all returned to the fire, and Dzhombe rose from the earth, turned to face the four directions of the wind, raised his arms to the mountains and cried to his men:

"Make your offerings to the earth!"

The fifteen men threw themselves at the girls, raping each one, spilling their seed into their bellies. Not until each girl had been ravished by each man did Dzhombe speak again, this time to the wizards.

"Complete the offering."

One by one the wizards took the bleeding girls to a place that had been prepared the week before. Into a trench dug in the earth they lay each girl down and prayed over her, begging the gods to accept their offering.

When all three were in the ditch, the men gathered above them and began to shove the moist, claylike earth on top of them. Numb from the *ganga* smoke and pain of their marriage rites, they tried to scream, but it was too late. Their thin legs were too weak to fight the weight of the earth being pushed on top of them.

The rites were complete. The earth would be reborn again by the seed of the men in the bodies of the brides.

Dzhombe's guards were on the alert at their posts when he returned. Saying nothing, Dzhombe went to a nearby stream and washed his body clean of its now streaked coat of ashes. Putting his uniform back on, he sat in the front seat of the weapons carrier and waited to be taken back to his capital. All was well, and the gods were pleased. It was time to return to the outside world, but he took with him, as always, a part of the old.

CHAPTER NINE

"Mr. Romain, I presume," said the Oxbridge-accented voice, his tone clearly meaning *I am a regular army officer and you are not*. Those exact words were unsaid, but the message was unmistakable. Casey and his men were distasteful to this graduate of Sandhurst, the British West Point that produced even stuffier officers than did its American counterpart. As with West Point alumni, once the new officers got the bullshit out of their brains, they were among the best military minds the world could produce, and if one didn't like their style, one couldn't argue with their sense of honor and personal courage. The British did do some things right, and training soldiers to be tough was one of them.

Casey stood in front of the officer with the full, bristling mustache and starched khaki drills, and said, once he got a look at the pips on the man's shoulders, "Major, I can tell right now that we may have some problems in communicating, so let's get it out in the open. I don't give a damn if you approve of me or my men, but we are here to do a job, and we're going to do it, even if it is the death of us"—he paused for a moment—"and you."

"Very good, Mr. Romain. You have made your position quite clear, and perhaps you're right. Incidentally, my name is Montfort. Your original contact assigned me to this job with orders to give you all the assistance you require, and in spite of any differences between us, that is exactly what I shall do. Now, if you will follow me, I will take you and your men to your quarters." He pointed across the landing strip to a cluster of Quonset huts. Casey told Beidemann to have Fitzhugh get the men and their gear, and follow him when they were ready.

As they crossed the strip, Montfort gave Casey the tourist-guide treatment. The field was set on a plain surrounded by low brush reaching out as far as the eye could see and spotted in places by giant baobab trees. Casey knew that in the trees and brush lived thousands of animals. Birds, lemurs, and leopards shared the baobabs. Lions and warthogs staked out their territories in the brush. A pair of vultures rode the hot air currents, rising from the flat runway to soar and glide in search of something dead or too weak to fight. Montfort pointed to them and said, "Not a bad omen, I hope." And he smiled.

"This, by the way, was an emergency field built by the South Africans during World War Two and used by them as a refueling depot on their way to the front in North Africa. At the far end of the runway there's one still usable hangar. That is where your advance cargo is stored. It has already been assembled. The field itself has been abandoned for the past twenty or so years, and now it's only used occasionally by hunters, ecologists, and the like. But with all the recent troubles, there are none of those types around now. I have ten of my own people here. They will act as a buffer between your people and anyone who might happen to stray this way. If that occurs, get your men out of sight and leave the talking to me. The reasons, I believe, are obvious."

Casey agreed.

"One more thing," said Montfort. "Meals will be served at 0600 hours, 1100, and at 1700."

"Just a moment, Major." Casey stopped, wiping the back of his hand across his forehead to get rid of the thin layer of red dust already collecting on it.

Montfort waited, watching his guest. "Yes? What is it?"

Lighting a cigarette between cupped hands, Casey took a drag and exhaled before speaking in flat tones. "We brought our own food, and we'll prepare it ourselves. Also, there will be no communication between your men and mine other than what is absolutely necessary."

"What is it, Mr. Romain?" Montfort responded a bit testily. "Do you think my men and our poor rations are not good enough for you and your overpaid prima donnas?"

Casey took a deep breath and got a grip on his temper.

"No, Major, but if you have served anyplace other than your own country and with anyone other than your own troops, you know that a change in diet can bring on dysentery and a number of other problems that could temporarily disable some of my men, and I have none to spare. This way they are used to the food and the way it is prepared." He ground out the cigarette butt under his heel.

"And I don't want any contact between your men and mine, because it could lead to short tempers and fights, which—if our own exchange is any example—will probably happen before supper."

By the time the conversation had reached this point, they had arrived at the old Quonset huts that would be their homes for the next week. Major Montfort chewed the ends of his sandy mustache as he thought over Casey's comments. "You're right, Mr. Romain," he admitted a bit reluctantly, "and I apologize. I am letting my personal prejudices against mercenaries color my thinking. You are right about the food and the troubles between our men. But remember this, sir. I am a professional soldier in the service of my country and will do anything to assure her survival. I fight for my home; you fight for money. That is what I find distasteful. For enough money you would fight against us."

Casey shook his head. "Montfort, if we had the time, I would tell you some things about us that might change your thinking, but it wouldn't make any difference to the mission, so let's just maintain a polite and friendly attitude and set an example for our men. And, incidentally, these 'prima donnas' of mine would bust your men open like watermelons just for the practice if they got pissed off. Like you said, you and your boys are patriots. Mine do this for a living. They have to be good or they wouldn't be here."

Casey turned his back on Montfort and entered the nearest hut, glad to be out of the sun, which was already gaining in strength. After meeting Montfort he wasn't surprised to see that the floors were clean. The GI-style bunks were made up with clean linen with blankets at the foot of each. Beidemann came in cursing, followed by George and the others. Fitzhugh was assigning bunks as Van set up their own security posts and duty roster.

As the men settled in, Casey, Beidemann, and George went for a look-see around the area just to get the feel of it and to work up a contingency plan in case anything went wrong while they were there.

Taking their time, they made a wide circle about a mile out so they could get a look at the field from the outside. Dust licked at the heels of their boots as lizards blinked out of their path to seek the small comfort of the shade of a bush. George didn't like what he saw. To him this was dead land, not having the rich soil of Southeast Asia, but he changed his mind when a warthog burst out of a clump of brush twenty feet ahead, hotly pursued by a young male lion who was just getting his mane. He didn't know who won the race. They disappeared down a dry wash to the south, the pig running with its tail stuck straight in the air and the young lion coming after him with long, space-eating leaps.

Casey let the others return to the Quonset huts, wanting to spend a few minutes by himself. Squatting down on his heels, he rested his chin on his forearms. Breathing deeply, he sucked into his lungs the hot, dry air of Africa. It would not always be dry. Soon the rains would come, and the veldt would come alive in a manner nearly beyond comprehension. The earth would erupt with vital green growth, and animals would pick this time to give birth to their young so they could grow strong before the next dry season set in.

To the north of them, in the deep jungle, there was not the dramatic change of season, just a time that was not quite so wet. And to the south and west lay the Kalahari, a place so dry it made the Mojave Desert look like a swamp.

A scorpion crept out of the roots of a bush, its pincers opening and closing as it scrambled within inches of Casey's feet. He ignored the tiny killer. He had seen them before, as he had a place such as this. In his mind's eye he could see the regiments of the Zulu tribes of the Matabele, the *impis* forming their battle lines in the shape of Cape buffalo horns. He saw the thousands of tall warriors of the Zulu wearing lion, civet, or black and white monkey fur, the fur strategically placed on their sweating ebony bodies or formed into fantastic headdresses. All chanted as they held their short spears, *iKwlas,* high over their heads.

Sweat collected in the small of his back and ran down his spine as the memory of the "horns of the buffalo," the tribal battle formation, advanced, singing and chanting. Hide shields of rhino or buffalo, painted with the totems of their clans, were held above their heads. The main force formed the base of the skull from which the horns tapered to a point, and the Zulus advanced upon the Boers. They had run forty miles for this fight, eager to wash their blades in blood. They advanced across the plain to the waiting Dutchmen in their circle of wagons and oxen. As they came closer, the points of the horns spread out in an arc as men flowed from the base, filling up the horns until they encircled their quarry. Ten thousand tall, proud warriors beat their shields and sang of their courage.

The Boers, tough, taciturn men with beards down to their chests, believing themselves to be the chosen of God and the servants of His Word, waited behind their wagons, rifles to their shoulders, hunting knives at their belts. Their wives stood with them, and as their children hid under or in the wagons ready to reload the rifles, they waited for the onslaught of the thousands of natives surrounding them. . . .

A shadow fell across him, jerking his mind back from that other, older Africa. Without turning to see, he asked softly, "What do you want, Major?"

Montfort paused as he watched the broad, muscled back below him. The sweat on the man's body had plastered his shirt to him like a second skin. Even under the cloth Montfort could see the great strength in that back; he watched the muscles ripple unconsciously, much as a horse's does as it shakes bothersome flies from its flank.

"Sorry to bother you, old boy. You looked like you were in deep thought, but your man Harrison wants to take a look at the Waco. My orders are that no one is to go near it until you say it is all right."

Grunting as he rose, the memory of that other time quickly faded into the past where it belonged.

"All right, let's go. By the way, what about the natives in this area?"

Montfort shrugged as he led the way through the brush back to the strip. "All the locals have been cleared out, and they won't be back for a while. We poisoned a number of their cattle and goats, then told them there was some kind of sickness for their animals in the area, and it would have to be quarantined for a time. They have all been moved to 'safe' areas until you are finished with your work. Then they'll be permitted to return."

Harrison met them on the runway, pointing toward

the old hangar. "I say, Casey, will you tell those louts over there——" he indicated two of the major's men who were standing guard at the hangar—"to let me into that bleedin' building? I can't fly the damned thing if I can't see it!"

Casey smiled at Harrison's normal annoyance at everything in the world. "Major Montfort, you may relieve your men. From this point on, my people will take responsibility for the security of the glider and our own equipment, which I am sure will suit you just fine."

Montfort grunted and called out to the two sentries, "You are relieved and will return to your quarters." Stamping their feet, the sentries saluted with rifles and trotted off.

Brushing a gnat away from the corner of his eye, Montfort started back across the field to where his own quarters were. He called back as he left, "I do hope you chaps will enjoy your stay here. Cheerie-o."

"Go bugger a camel, you overstuffed arsehole!" Harrison muttered under his breath.

Casey grabbed Harrison by the arm and directed him to the hangar door. "Don't give me any trouble. I don't want to have a harder time dealing with Montfort than I'm having already. Just keep your wisecracks to yourself for the time being and do your job. Report to me after dinner if you have any problems."

As usual, Harrison felt that he was being unfairly chastised and just put Casey's misunderstanding of him down to an obviously common education. Opening the door to the hangar, he had second thoughts and made excuses in his mind for Casey's treatment of him. Feeling better, he went in.

CHAPTER TEN

Six days to go. Not much time, but it was best that way. The men were becoming short-tempered and edgy. Beidemann and Fitzhugh noticed the change and started to work their asses off. They knew they couldn't risk leaving the men idle for too long or the situation would become explosive. They were too close to the staging area. Their subconscious fears were beginning to show. Some smoked more, others lost their appetites, and then there were those who picked fights. But Beidemann and Fitzhugh worked them so hard they had no time to let fear eat at them, and when they hit the sack at night they slept straight through until reveille. From dawn to dusk

the two officers ran the men through live fire exercises
and ten- and fifteen-mile forced marches with full packs
until the sweat drying on their jackets turned white with
the salts they'd leached out. At the end of each day,
Fitzhugh and Beidemann reported to Casey, who was
satisfied with their work. Several fights were brought to
a halt when Fitzhugh and Beidemann offered to take on
anyone who felt froggy enough to jump. The German's
size and strength were such that there were no takers,
and all the mercs knew that Fitzhugh was the better
soldier. Though he might piss them off, what he made
them do was designed for their own survival and they
knew it. If anyone pushed him too hard, he'd cheerfully
put a bullet into the back of that man's neck with Casey's
approval. There could be no weak links in this chain of
men. Each accomplished his job in his own way. There
was grumbling, which was to be expected, but no major
discipline problems arose.

Only Harrison was excused from most of the training
exercises, but even he had to make the forced marches.
About that, Casey was firm. He'd been on too many
operations where the unexpected happened too frequently
to take any chances. If anything went wrong and they
weren't able to get airlifted out of the site after hitting
Dzhombe, then they'd need their legs more than they
would ammo. Harrison bitched about it, but like the
others, he knew the reasons for it. Except for the marches,
his time was spent in the single hangar going over the
old Waco glider. Each strut was checked and some were
reinforced; the canvas was poked and prodded as he
searched out dry rot. Any spot that didn't meet with his
total approval was replaced. Every bolt, gear, and guy
line was oiled. He spent hours in the cockpit making his

own dry runs. Closing his eyes, he'd try to visualize the flight and everything that could go wrong. A hundred times he landed the glider in his mind. He would have loved to have taken the plane up just once to feel her out, but if anything happened to her on takeoff or landing, they'd be up the creek when the time came to make the strike. Any tests would have to be made in the air, and there was only one place the glider would set down: Matthew Dzhombe's presidential palace grounds.

Major Montfort had to admit that the hirelings were good, *very* good. He watched their training with a knowing eye. He didn't like it much, but it was obvious that what Casey Romain had said about his men was the absolute truth. As good as his own soldiers were, they'd have had little chance in a firefight or hand-to-hand combat situation against the mercs.

On the fifth day, after a single-engine Cessna made a quick stop and turn-around, Montfort presented himself with an attaché case at the small room to the rear of one of the Quonset huts, where Casey had his office set up. Knocking on the door, he waited for permission to enter.

"Come in, Major." As Montfort turned the handle on the door, he wondered how Casey always seemed to know who it was that was behind him, or as now, outside his door.

Casey sat behind a card table that served as a desk. He was going over aerial maps of Kimshaka City and the surrounding countryside. Not rising, he indicated the single metal folding chair in front of the card table. "Have a seat, Major. I'll be with you in just a moment."

For the five-hundredth time he went over the layout of the palace and surrounding grounds. Putting down the magnifying glass he'd been using, he turned his attention to his guest. "Yes, Major? What can I do for you?"

Montfort opened the attaché case without rising, took out a sealed manila envelope, and handed it across the card table to Casey. "These just came in by courier. I believe they're what you've been waiting for."

Casey slit open the flap. "I hope so." Removing the contents, he spread them out on the table. Rifling through them quickly, he took a fast look and then set them aside, saying in flat, noncommittal tones, "Is there anything else I can do for you?"

Montfort accepted his dismissal with good grace, knowing full well that what Casey was doing was exercising his right of a man's having a need to know. Montfort didn't need to know the contents of the envelope.

Rising from the chair, he smoothed an imaginary wrinkle in his shirt. "No, that's all for now. But I do want you to know that I wish you and your men the best of luck. Your mission is as important to me as it is to anyone else in my country, and while we may have our differences, a lack of respect for your group's capabilities is not one of them. I'll be close by if you need anything from me."

Casey was a little surprised at the major's comments, and he made a mental note to buy the stuffy officer a drink when and if they got back.

Walking to the doorway, Casey yelled for Fitzhugh. Fitzhugh answered his summons by presenting himself with a proper British salute. "Sir!" he said, stamping his right foot.

"Get Gus, Van, Harrison, and George. All of you report to me ASAP." Stamping both feet, Fitzhugh about-faced and strode off with that peculiarly British manner of marching where the fists swung out nearly to chest level.

It took less than half an hour to get them all together in the small room. Van opened the windows wide to let in a bit more air while the others found chairs and stools to sit on.

Distributing the contents of the manila envelope, Casey had each one go over the pages. George didn't read English too well, but he'd pick up more than enough from the conversation. The papers were passed around until all had a chance to give them at least a cursory inspection. Then they went over the details.

Taking each man's questions one at a time, they went over the new input: the location and number of Simbas in the capital; the location of guard posts and checkpoints; the motor pools and available civilian vehicles if needed; the number of Simbas on regular duty at the palace and their armament. Most of Dzhombe's soldiers were outfitted with AK-47s donated by Kimshaka's once friendly advisor, the Soviet Union. Heavy weapons were from the same family: RPD light machine guns and a few PKS 7.62mm crew-served machine guns on tripods. These and a few mortars of varying calibers were kept inside the palace armory along with some other heavy weaponry, including a few American-made 57mm recoilless rifles.

The location of Dzhombe's rooms was clearly indicated in charts showing the entire floor plan of the palace building. A timetable showed the schedule of events of the last time Dzhombe had celebrated his ascendance to power, and there was a list of guests known or expected to be in attendance at the festivities to take place the day after tomorrow.

With his squad leaders Casey discussed the routes out
of town and the alternates in case they ran into resistance
too stiff to reduce on their primary route. He pointed out
on the maps where the alternate rendezvous sites were
located. This was done so that if anyone became separated from the main party, he'd know where to go and
how to make contact with the N.F.L.K. Another page
contained the colors of the flares and radio codes to be
used to identify themselves to the N.F.L.K. if they were
needed. The success of the operation depended on Matthew Dzhombe's history.

For the last five years, after Dzhombe gave his State
of Kimshaka speech, a drunken orgy had taken place at
the palace. Even the troops not on duty ended up smashed.

Many of the festivities had always taken place in the
palace garden, which was ringed by strings of colored
lights. Those lights would guide them in.

Asking for final critiques from his men and receiving
none, Casey said, "Okay, gentlemen, that's the way it
goes down. Each of you will return to me tomorrow
morning for final instructions pertaining to your separate
missions. Give the men tomorrow afternoon off. Let
them relax and sleep if they can. They may need it later.
We pull out at 1700 hours. Remove all signs of our
presence here. Clean up the area. I want it sterilized."

Van and the others went out into the Quonset huts,
gathering their men to them to pass along the orders and
to answer any questions.

Afterward, when night fell, George sat quietly sharp-
ening his blade, then he cleaned his shotgun. Van lay
on his bunk thinking of the Chinese girl working at Raffles in Singapore. Casey heard Beidemann sit down on
a folding chair outside his hut and then begin to sing
softly: *Wann wir beide Laterne stehn, wie einst, Lili*

Marlene, wie einst Lili Marlene?" Another voice joined that of the giant German. Fitzhugh added his own words to the famous song of another war: "Underneath the lantern by the barrack gate, Darling, I remember the way you used to wait; 'Twas there that you whispered tenderly, That you'd love me..."

Good men. Steady. They'd be where they were needed, Casey thought, listening to them. He tried not to think about those who would probably be dead by this time tomorrow, even though he understood that they knew the risks and each had his own reasons for taking them....

Casey walked out past the sentry, telling him that he'd be gone for a time. He felt the need to be by himself. Walking into the bush just far enough so he felt the solitude he needed, he sat down on a half-rotten log that the termites hadn't yet finished with and opened up the buttons of his shirt, letting the night's mild breeze evaporate the moisture from his hot flesh. It felt good.

Cupping his hands to shield the flame of his lighter, he lit up. The deceptive quiet of the night didn't fool him. He knew that hundreds of thousands of creatures were out there in the dark, feeding on each other, breeding, dying. He wasn't alone. He had long since given up trying to make any sense out of his life. *Life,* he thought as he sucked the ash into a bright orange glow. *What is life without death? How can anything have a meaning that doesn't have an ending?*

Grinding the butt out, he heard a hunting lionness announce that she and her pride would eat tonight. The proud roar of the victorious killer could easily be heard for miles over the veldt. What was it Van had once said to him? "What more can a man do than to pick his time and place to die?"

That's what all the others with him were doing. But

for him . . . His time for that pleasure still lay somewhere in the unforeseeable future. He almost didn't believe in himself anymore. It had been so long that even his own reality was subject to his own disbelief. Several times he had thought he'd gone mad and that his existence was merely the nightmares of a diseased mind. No such luck. Madness would have been a kindness. As always, he had no choice but to continue on, hoping against hope that one day he would hear the words that would grant him peace.

A figure concealed in the darkness waited for him by the hangar. "Hello, Major. What keeps you up this late?"

Montfort cursed under his breath. *How does he do that?*

"Oh, not much, old boy. Just came by to once again wish you the best. I know you'll probably be quite busy tomorrow." He coughed a bit self-consciously as he said what he didn't think he was capable of. "By the by, when you get back, what say we go out for a drink and dinner?"

Casey grinned in the dark. "I was going to ask you the same thing, Major. Thanks, I think I'd like that very much."

Montfort cleared his throat again. "Have you ever thought about emigrating to a country like ours? You know, this would be a place where you could be very comfortable. If you did decide on such a course, I would be—that is if you wished—I would be very glad to do what I could to see about getting you a commission in the regular army." Casey smiled at the man's attempt at creating a friendship.

"Thanks for the offer, Major. Tell you what. Let's talk about it when I get back. Right now might be a bit premature."

Montfort bobbed his head up and down. "Of course, of course. We shall do that by all means. Well, if you'll excuse me, I have a few things of my own to take care of before calling it a night. See you tomorrow, Mr. Romain." Before leaving, he gave Casey a number to call when he returned.

CHAPTER ELEVEN

Two planes, one with its umbilical cord attached to the Waco, droned their way through the night, rising over whispy columns of clouds. Beneath, the plains of the veldt gave way to the darker growth of the tropical jungle.

The transport aircraft carrying the jumpers was an American C-119 that should have been retired from service ten years earlier but somehow always held together so it could make one more flight. A C-47 of even more ancient vintage was assigned as the tow aircraft for the Waco. It would be two minutes behind the C-119.

The men were silent as they boarded the transport.

Fitzhugh and George were with Casey in the C-119. Van and Harrison were in the glider with the heavy weapons section, along with Beidemann and his unit. Their gear was secured with straps to keep it from breaking loose when they touched down.

Beside Casey, George sat unconcerned, not really caring where he went as long as his friends were with him. That was enough. And these black Cong he was going to kill could not be too different from the others in Vietnam and Cambodia.

For Casey, the remaining hours until they reached the drop zone were spent going over the final plans again and again, trying to anticipate everything that could possibly go wrong. Reviewing the plan, it seemed simple enough. Their aircraft would be coming in on the same flight path that a regularly scheduled flight from Pretoria used at this time every week, but the regular flight would be delayed for thirty minutes while the mercs' plane took its place. The troops in Kimshaka were used to the regular commercial flights and wouldn't be alarmed at the sound of the transport's engines. Nor would the air traffic controllers behind their radarscopes in the airfield tower think anything was out of the ordinary. They would be given the proper call signs and would think the plane was just a bit off course as it made its approach to the field. How the white Africans had arranged for the delay was none of his business.

Harrison sat calmly at the controls of the glider, taking it easy. He kept a light hand on the stick, letting the tow aircraft do the work. So far, so good. The old Waco handled quite well and was riding steady.

Beidemann came up front and sat in the copilot's seat. Below, the jungle was bathed in a bluish glow. Soon the moon would be down. They had another four hours until they would be cut loose. In the back, the men were preparing themselves again; for the tenth time they made last checks of themselves and their gear. They had changed into tiger-striped camouflage uniforms, stuffing their civvies into a duffel bag.

At the same time as the C-119 and C-47 carried their cargoes of death through the night skies of Africa, the liberation forces of Kimshaka were ambushing small government outposts around the capital, drawing off troops from the city until even the palace guard had to send out most of their off-duty men to take care of these insect bites that threatened to spoil the gaiety of the Avenging Lion's celebration.

News of these raids were kept from Field Marshal Dzhombe. They were not serious. No positions had been lost. They were only nuisance actions designed to interrupt the festivities and embarrass their leader. A wise man knew when not to bother Matthew Dzhombe with bad news. In the morning it would all be over with anyway, so why disturb the master?

The men in the C-119 adjusted the straps on their parachutes; the damned things never seemed to fit exactly right. Most of the men felt as if they had to take a leak, a common phenomenon when a person's under stress. The body wants to eliminate fluid in the bladder when danger is near. That way, if the body is injured, the risk of severe infection from a urine-filled, ruptured bladder is reduced.

The pilot left his seat in the C-119 and went back to speak to Casey.

"You have one hour to go to the DZ. If there's anything you or your men need to do, you'd better do it now. Once we get near the drop zone, my copilot will come back and act as jumpmaster for you. Don't worry about him. He's had over a thousand free falls and knows his business. Nothing but the best for you guys." His voice was steady, with just a hint of the American Midwest in it.

"You're an American," said Casey, surprised.

"That's right. Dayton, Ohio. Don't ask what I'm doing up here and I won't ask you, okay?"

"Okay," replied Casey with a broad grin, pulling himself up from the canvas bucket seat. The pilot returned to his controls, and Casey yelled out over the noise of the engines, "One hour to go. Check your weapons and your harness. Make sure there are no grenades hanging loose that can catch on something. Keep them off your webbing and in your bags until we exit the plane."

The Midwestern voice turned on the interior red lights so the mercs could see what they were doing and to give their eyes time to adjust to the darkness outside. The red glow gave a strange, hellish aura to everyone and everything it touched. The interior of the plane could have been a scene out of Dante's *Inferno*. The night bird flew on. . . .

Field Marshal and Premier for Life, Matthew Dzhombe sat on the hereditary throne of his tribe and held court. His speech of the day had been hailed by one and all as his best, and no one seemed to mind the four and a half hours it took to deliver. The thundering cheers of the people assured him of their devotion, especially since his best troops, his ufaSimbas, were covering them with automatic weapons. No one seemed to notice when some Simbas took away several spectators. Included in this group were a number of attractive young women. No one interfered. Their fate was well known, and not all of the young women were frightened. Some thought it could be a way to a better life if they pleased Dzhombe.

Cars waited to take them to the palace for the pleasure of Dzhombe and his guests. Once there, they would be bathed, dressed in gowns from Europe, and given instructions as to their duties. All obeyed. To refuse was unthinkable.

The celebrations at the presidential palace had started soon after Dzhombe's speech had ended and the huge crowd was permitted to return to their homes. No stores or restaurants were open for business. Everyone was to be in his own house by nightfall. Anyone found on the streets without special permission would be shot on the spot.

The party at the palace had degenerated into its normal drunken orgy. Dzhombe roared with laughter, his huge frame shaking with mirth, as his sycophants enjoyed his bounty. The pretty young women brought in for the celebration laughed too, most of them high. Cocaine, heroin, and hashish were to be had for the asking. Possession of narcotics was a crime only when Matthew Dzhombe said it was.

The palace grounds were lit with lanterns, the walls adorned with strings of multicolored bulbs. Many of the guests had already passed out or were clutching each other in the bushes and flower gardens. Dzhombe's few remaining off-duty palace guards helped themselves to whatever they could get their hands on. Dzhombe, they knew, understood their needs, and as long as they didn't offend anyone of importance, they could do as they pleased.

Dzhombe watched over them, resembling some gross idol observing his worshipers in their pagan rites. Nothing escaped him. He made a mental note of those he did not like. His criteria for this fatal judgment was often nothing more than that the subject of his displeasure did not seem to be enjoying himself enough. Sober men who avoided healthy whores at his parties were men to be watched. Before selecting for himself one of the women who had been taken from the streets, he made one last scan of the doorways and windows. The men there were not drinking. All were completely sober, trying to be unobtrusive as they watched over their master's guests. Each Simba's rifle was loaded and ready to fire.

Clanggggg! The ten-minute warning bell rang, startling in its suddenness. Casey stood and hooked up, giving the command to his men to do the same. As they lined up, he yelled out over the plane's roar, "Sound off!" Starting at the rear of the first stick came the responses:

"Thirty okay."

"Twenty-nine okay."

"Twenty-eight okay . . ."

Casey was number one. All of them would be out of the plane in less than twenty seconds from the time the jumpmaster gave the word. Both sticks would exit by the tail. They'd be jumping at about seven hundred feet. No reserves were carried. If anything went wrong, there'd be no time to use one anyway. From that jump height, they would be in the air for only about twenty-three seconds before they touched down. That wouldn't give Dzhombe's guards much time to respond to the invasion.

"One minute to the DZ," came the call from the copilot now turned jumpmaster, a tough-looking man in his thirties wearing British and American jump wings on his olive-drab coveralls. He pulled the switch that opened the tailgate, exposing the night to the men inside. Then he opened the side door and stuck his head out to check on their approach. When the tailgate opened, a rush of wind whirled through the red-lit interior, a welcome bit of relief in the claustrophobic confines of the flying box-car.

Casey's men got ready, hands on their static lines. They'd tucked their soft caps into pockets where they wouldn't be lost during the jump and tightened the chin straps on the British-made paratroop helmets, the kind that resembled motorcycle helmets more than anything else.

The lights of Kimshaka City were clearly visible to the jumpmaster as he gauged their distance. The C-119 had finished making its descent and had leveled off at seven hundred feet.

"Stand in the door," came the jumpmaster's command. Casey moved forward to the lip of the tailgate. Below him he could see the lights of individual houses and cooking fires. He wished that he'd been able to get a look at where they were heading, but he'd have to leave that to the jumpmaster's discretion and trust that the man was right.

Behind him, all were tense. A mixture of anticipation and fear ran through their bodies like an electric current.

"*Go!*" At the jumpmaster's order, Casey stepped out into the black night. Putting one foot over the edge of the tail, he was well aware that the next step was seven hundred feet down. Then he brought his other up to meet it and fell, his elbows tucked in, hands holding his kit bag close to his chest where his reserve chute would have been had he had one.

He was out and falling, his body whipped back by

the cyclone blast of the C-119's props. There was a deafening roar followed by the opening shock of the chute. At the same time, the world went silent as the plane flew on ahead. Quickly he checked his risers, then looked around the sky for his men. They were all there. Turning his chute, he saw that the jumpmaster had been exactly on target; the palace grounds were directly below. The strings of colored lights on the walls serving as their marker, the mercs guided their chutes down.

Squinting his eyes, he saw several Simbas staring up at the chutes falling at them from the night sky. The ground came up almost faster than he could get ready for it. He hit hard, but nothing broke. Rolling over and hitting his quick release to break free of his chute harness, he unslung his Swedish M45 submachine gun and went down on one knee. The others were landing all around him.

A drunken soldier ran up to him, grinning, a hand extended with a bottle of Johnny Walker Red in it, the black man offering Casey a drink. The grin was stopped by the smashing of the Simba's jawbone with the metal stock of the gun.

Simbas started to yell out warnings, and several of the guests began to get a look of terror in their glazed eyes as they realized this was not some bizarre form of entertainment that their master had arranged for their amusement.

George ran up to kneel beside Casey, his sawed-off shotgun at the ready. A group of five guards broke from the bushes to their right. One struggled with the bolt of his rifle. The time had come.

Not speaking, Casey took out the far two with a short, three-round burst, twice repeated. The thundering sound of George's twelve-gauge terminated the other three, blasting them back fifteen feet before they hit the ground. The fight was on.

Casey's mercs got their act together and started knocking out the guard posts on the garden walls. Two men had run to the garden gate where any reinforcements for the Simbas would have to enter. They took up positions on each side and waited. Their job was to keep the garden secure. Three minutes had elapsed. The mercs held the courtyard, but the Simbas were beginning to organize and return fire. Several of the mercs were wounded. Only one was dead, a young Irishman.

Casey gathered some men and assaulted the doorway, gaining the interior. They were brought to a halt by a blocking force of ten palace guards who had placed themselves to cover the entrance to the palace from the garden grounds. They were well protected behind columns and balustrades, and were beginning to lay down effective fire. Another merc went down, his face a shattered wreck from the burst of an AK-47 on full automatic.

Turning to the south, Casey muttered, "Where the hell is that limey?"

Then suddenly it was there. The number two aircraft had cut her loose and banked off to port. The glider was silently floating in and down . . . four hundred, three hundred, two hundred . . . and then, raising her nose, Harrison tail-dragged the old bird into the shallow pond, scaring the shit out of two nude couples fooling around near the water who'd remained oblivious to the sounds of gunfire around them. The sight of the giant bird falling silently toward them was too much for the girls, who promptly screamed and dove under the water to get away.

One man, Kimshaka's minister of culture, had his

head taken off as he just stood there staring as if he couldn't believe what was happening. The Waco was down and splashing to a halt, the starboard wing torn off as she hit a clump of small trees. She slid out of the water and stopped about twenty yards behind Casey and about thirty from the palace.

Inside, the men were tossed from side to side, and one man's arm snapped at the elbow when he was thrown into the 57mm recoilless rifle. Swearing, he thrust his broken arm between his combat webbing straps and kicked the door open before the bird had come to a complete stop. Pulling his pistol, he shot a Simba in the face. The merc leaped to the ground and started looking for targets. He was followed by Van, who quickly had his team set up their mortars and had the recoilless rifle taken to where Casey and George were directing fire on the rear doors and porches of the palace.

Seven minutes had passed since Casey had landed in the courtyard. Van smiled, showing even, white teeth in his handsome face. "Yes, master, this boy will get to work right now."

Loading the 57mm rifle with a high explosive round, Van blew up the group of Simbas who had rushed to defend the palace entrance, ripping them into pieces that would take a master at jigsaw puzzles to put together again for their funerals.

"Too long!" Casey cried. "It's taking too long! We've got to get inside!" Leaving three men outside to keep the Simbas occupied, he took George with him and ran into Beidemann coming at them with a rope and grappling hook slung over his shoulder. No dialogue was necessary.

The old German whirled the hook around his head,

tossing it up onto the balcony of a room on the second floor. Not waiting for orders, he was up the line like a bear up a tree trunk. He was followed by George, then Casey. Van had reloaded his rifle and was aiming it at the Simbas at the rear door. Casey called down for him to get on with it. While they were still on the second floor porch, they heard the whooshing blast of the recoilless rifle as Van cut loose with a canister round into the palace interior.

Casey kicked open the porch door and tumbled inside. No one was there to stop them, just two frightened women who hid their faces behind their hands and begged him not to kill them. Beidemann and George were on his heels, and the German beat him to the door leading to the second floor hallway. Stepping out first, he cut down two Simbas who had their backs turned to him. They'd been watching the action downstairs.

Beidemann and George began laying down some fire support to their men below. Between them they reduced the return fire of the enemy by fifty percent in less than twenty seconds. Screams came from every corner of the palace as the panicked guests sought shelter. Several of them, including a few women, were cut down when they ran into crossfire between the mercs and the Simbas.

Yelling downstairs, Casey ordered Fitzhugh to hold the ground floor and see that the escape group got over to the motor pool to commandeer any vehicles they could get their hands on. Fitzhugh gave a regulation salute and began barking out orders to that effect.

Knowing Fitzhugh would see things done properly, Casey and his crew raced up the next flight of stairs to the third floor. Beidemann shot someone who stuck his head out of a bedroom door. At a time like that, he couldn't wait to see if the person was going to be sociable or not. At the head of the third floor staircase, three of Dzhombe's elite guard were waiting, stone cold sober and ready. They were the ones who had been privileged to accompany their master back to his home kraal. They were the faithful hounds guarding their master's door.

As the mercenaries hit the top, the guards began to fire. Beidemann was creased along the inside of his thigh. Cursing in three languages, he sprayed the hallway along with the others. The three sentries absorbed over eighty bullets and several shotgun slugs.

Casey's gun was empty. Not taking time to change magazines, he pulled his pistol from its holster and blew out the lock on the right side of the large double doors behind which they hoped to find Matthew Dzhombe. Giving the door a kick with his foot, it swung open. Jumping back against the side of the hallway, he expected some kind of response from the man inside.

There was nothing for a few seconds. Then a heavy voice boomed out, "Who disturbs me?" The question was repeated, this time the volume approaching that of an angry bull elephant.

Cautiously glancing around the edge of the doorway, the mercenaries peeked in. Dzhombe was rising from his bed, a giant gargoyle. Stark naked, his blue-black skin glistened with oil and sweat. The shooting outside had penetrated his consciousness. The bhang he had eaten had separated his mind from reality, taking him to another plateau of awareness that blocked out the everyday world. The woman lying under him had been screaming as he'd taken her, using her as an object of sacrifice to his gods and himself. The screams had been to him only her acceptance of the state of grace she was entering. The fact that his sex organs were in direct proportion to his size and had torn her apart meant nothing to him. The screams and blood from the woman were normal for him, expected, indeed almost needed. . . .

The mercs were stunned for a moment by this nightmarish apparition. The photos they'd seen of the man didn't prepare them for his true size and his aura of primitive, brutal power.

Casey had no time to waste. Stepping inside the door, he fired twice with his pistol, hitting Dzhombe in the stomach with both rounds. The slugs knocked him back, and Dzhombe laughed through a bhang-induced anesthesia. Moving beside Casey, Beidemann fired a three-round burst from his G-3, knocking Dzhombe to the floor. At such close range they could clearly hear the bullets slapping into the man's body. Dzhombe, favored of the gods and inheritor of the Kingdom of Shaka, rolled back up from the floor to his feet. He quivered for a moment, then shook his body, whipping a spray of sweat and blood all over the room.

Staggering to regain his balance, he laughed, bloody foam bubbling from his lips. "Fools," he gurgled. The gaping holes in his chest and back seemed not to give him any pain at all.

"Fools, you cannot kill me. Only the gods have that right. I am their child, Shaka, born again into the body of Matthew Dzhombe."

The mercs stopped firing. Even Casey was stunned by what he was witnessing. Dzhombe should have been dead, but there he stood, laughing at them, his hide glistening with sweat and blood, not only from the gunshot wounds but also from the woman who still lay on the bed sobbing in pain.

Dzhombe threw back his head and screamed. It wasn't a scream of fear or pain, but one of rage. For a moment the sound even halted the gunfire outside. "I am a child of the gods! They protect me," he bellowed.

George had seen just about enough. He pushed his way between Beidemann and Casey, leveled the bore of the twelve-gauge shotgun, and fired two rounds. Both hit their target, lifting Dzhombe from his feet and throwing him against the bedroom wall. Dzhombe didn't fall even though the shotgun had torn off his left elbow and ripped open the madman's rib cage to where the internal organs were exposed between the bloody, torn flap of skin and bone hanging down to his hips.

The men in the doorway held their fire, amazed that their target wasn't down. Each had killed many times before, but never had they seen anything like this. What was the force that could keep this giant of a man on his feet? They knew they were witnessing a sight they would never see again.

Dzhombe was a dead man; he just didn't know it. His mind could not accept being killed by ordinary mortals. The voices of his childhood were speaking to him again, calling to him. Dzhombe's eyes grew wide as he stared at the doorway leading to the outside balcony.

Joruba, the feathered messenger of the gods, stood there. It was Joruba who had brought fire to man and took the spirits of the scar-faced back to the gods who lived in the mountains to the north. Joruba beckoned to Dzhombe, his right hand holding a flaming torch, the symbol of the gods' great gift to man.

"Come," said the hollow voice of the messenger, his face hidden behind a mask of carved ebony. "Come, son of Shaka. You have been accepted. Come and join us.

It is time for you to become one with us. Come and be a god."

Dzhombe roared with laughter. Reaching out, he took a short *iKwla,* a stabbing spear, from the wall where it hung beside a ceremonial shield of buffalo hide. The mercs backed up, still not firing, almost hypnotized by what was occurring.

Dzhombe held the spear above his head, blood pouring freely from his wounds, startlingly white bone mixed with red muscle and black skin. Crimson pools of his life formed around his feet.

"Did you hear?" He spoke the words as if the men trying to kill him were dear friends and not his executioners. "Did you hear?" he repeated, coughing up big gouts of blood from his lungs. "They want me, Dzhombe, the soul of Shaka, to be one of them. I am a god. I am going to join my brothers who wait for me in the great mountains."

For the first time since they had arrived, Dzhombe seemed to take real notice of the men at his door and their weapons. Stepping forward a pace, he wavered, caught himself, and pointed the *iKwla* at them. "Do you fools think a mortal can kill a god? No, you cannot. Your guns cannot take what belongs to the heavens or set my spirit free to join my brothers. It takes a god to kill a god." Matthew Dzhombe laughed hysterically and repeated, "It takes a god to kill a god!"

Dzhombe waved the ragged stump of his left arm in the air, showering the room with a rain of blood. Still laughing, he shifted his grip to the head of the spear. Whirling around in a circle, he drove the three-foot blade into his chest. Grasping the handle with his good hand, he tried to force the blade all the way in, but he couldn't.

The steel was stuck in the heavy bones and thick muscles of his chest. The blood he had lost took away the strength needed to finish the job. He stopped his spinning and looked at the faces of the men watching him. Red-rimmed and mad, his eyes searched the face of each man. There was one there who might understand. Pointing with his stump, he commanded the scar-faced, gray-eyed mercenary, "You! You are the one to assist me. Hurry!"

Casey stuffed his pistol into his belt. He knew what Dzhombe wanted. When he started forward, the others didn't stop him. They were no longer part of this ritual. Casey stood beside the bloody giant. He could smell the thick odor of blood and sex mixed with that of coming death. Dzhombe held out his good hand and took Casey's, placing it on the haft of the spear.

Conversationally, between lung-ripping coughs, Dzhombe said, "You are the one. You know what has to be done." Casey said nothing. Gripping the haft with both hands, he waited until Dzhombe replaced his own hand near the head of the spear, then began to push, twisting the blade until it broke free of the bone holding it. Dzhombe grinned at him. "Good, now the rest..." Three hands grasped the weapon, and as one they pushed and pulled, forcing the *iKwla* a foot out of Dzhombe's back.

Casey released his grip and stepped back. The rest of what was to happen was for Dzhombe alone to finish. Dzhombe turned to the open doorway.

Joruba waited for him. The mask of the spirit smiled at him. Taking his hand, Joruba intoned, "You have done well. Now, come with me." Holding Joruba's hand, Matthew Dzhombe flew to the mountains. Matthew Dzhombe, born-again soul of Shaka, Avenging Lion of Kimshaka, had become one with his brothers.

The mercenaries rushed to the balcony and looked down at Dzhombe's body, which had crashed over the railing and fell to the courtyard three floors below. They were still in a state of shock from what they had seen take place in the premier's room. A tinge of fear ran through them all, even Casey.

A Simba wearing the stripes of a sergeant on his comouflage jacket saw Dzhombe's body fall. He sent up a cry. "The Lion is dead! The Lion is dead!"

The remaining Simbas broke and ran. They had no heart to fight anymore. Dzhombe was gone. They were lost without him, and they knew that others would be coming soon to take their revenge on those who had supported him. They ran out of the palace through the darkened streets to their barracks, where they might find safety in numbers. They knew the killing had not ended with the death of their master. Now they would have to fight for their lives against those they had ruled over in the name of Matthew Dzhombe, and there were many, many scores that would be settled in the next few days. . . .

CHAPTER TWELVE

In the palace courtyard, the mercs wiped up what feeble, demoralized resistance remained. They took a number of prisoners, disarmed them, and locked them up in one of the palace storerooms. As Casey and the others came down from Dzhombe's rooms, they had to step over the bodies of Simbas and the distinguished guests who'd died in their master's house. A fire had started somewhere in the rear of the palace, but they had neither the time nor the interest to put it out.

Harrison called to them from the seat of a half-track. He'd gone with Fitzhugh to the palace's motor pool. His new acquisition was American-made, and behind it came Fitzhugh, driving a British Saladin armored car on which was mounted a 20mm gun. One more half-track pulled up with Yousef standing behind a captured Russian RPD light machine gun. Casey wondered where he'd been and figured that the Moroccan had attached himself to Harrison during the melee. One other vehicle, a two-and-a-half-ton open-bed truck, made up the vehicles for their escape.

Waving them aboard, Casey yelled to all not to leave any of the gear behind, which included his MG-34 still in its drop bag. The light machine gun hadn't been needed during the fight, but they weren't out of danger yet. There was still the escape from the city to be made, and they could run into enemy patrols. Fitzhugh and Harrison gunned the engines of the vehicles. The operation had now been on the ground for forty-three minutes; they should be gone. As they loaded, Casey put the casualties into the truck and positioned it between the Saladin and the last half-track. They had gotten off fairly easy: four dead and six wounded, only one critically. The medic was already working on the badly injured man.

Guns pointing to the outside, the mercenaries loaded up and headed out into the streets of Kimshaka City, turning down the main thoroughfare and aiming for the lines of the N.F.L.K. about ten miles south, near the Soruba River.

Word of Dzhombe's death had preceded them. From some houses came the sounds of panic and sorrow; in others there was rejoicing that the monster was gone. Already, Dzhombe's officers were drawing the lines to see who would inherit his power. The mercs drove as fast as they could while keeping all the vehicles close enough to each other to give mutual support in case it was needed. A number of Simbas, still in shock at the news, wandered the streets, randomly shooting out windows of whitewashed, flat-roofed buildings and shanties made of tin sheeting. A couple of them took a few shots at the vehicles, but they were quickly cut down by the mercs' automatic weapons. Leaving the lights of the capital behind, in less than ten minutes they entered the first thin line of trees and brush. The time on site was now exactly one hour and three minutes.

The men felt good. Things had gone pretty much as planned, although the manner of Dzhombe's death had caused some excitement and speculation as to what it sometimes took to kill a man. But he was dead, and that was what mattered. Now all they had to do was get to the lines of the N.F.L.K., and they were home free.

As they rode, magazines were refilled from boxes of loose ammo, and weapons were checked to make certain that everything was in good working order. The men had all been around too long not to know that as long as they were on the ground in enemy country, anything could happen. The survivors of these kinds of operations were the ones who didn't take unnecessary chances or get careless at the last moment when all appeared to be safe and secure.

Sitting with Harrison in the shotgun seat of the lead half-track, Casey looked over his map by the glow of a flashlight and told the Englishman to bear to the right at the next fork in the road. So far they had been riding on blacktop, which would end at the fork. The half-track had seen better days—probably right after World War II—but the engine still seemed sound and ran well enough to please Harrison. At the split in the road, Casey had Harrison pull over and stop. The other vehicles came to a halt in a line behind them, their passengers wary, guns pointing out on all sides. Those in the armored vehicles kept their bodies shielded behind the steel sides of their transport.

Stepping out and stretching, Casey removed a flare gun from one of the kit bags Harrison had put in the front seat. Selecting the proper shells, he loaded and fired a red then a green flare into the sky. Watching the flares flame over the trees like beacons from a ship at sea, they slowly faded to nothing as they fell to earth. Two, then three minutes passed and there it was! One white flare answering theirs.

"Everyone back on board! And keep your eyes open— we're not out of this yet! When we get to the next turn in the road, watch for me to blink my lights. Yousef, you unpack my MG and put a drum on it. Van, you hang back with Fitzhugh in his half-track and keep out of sight. Keep your heavy stuff ready. Set up a mortar in the bed of your vehicle and place the fifty-seven millimeter so you can fire from the front without any of your people getting blown away by the back blast. If anything comes down wrong, get your ass in high gear and bail us out. Got it?"

Van acknowledged his orders. "Got it, master. This boy always ready to do white god's bidding," Van said, teasing him, his boyish smile making him look more like a teenager than a battle-proven soldier.

Casey grinned back and muttered something about an insubordinate little bastard.

Slowly they started off. Fitzhugh turned off his lights and let the others get far enough ahead so their taillights would just be visible. In the rear, Van got his gear ready as Casey had ordered and leaned out over the cab to the front, eyes squinting to catch any movement. The half-tracks and the British Saladin were doing only about eighteen miles an hour, taking their time as they headed in the direction from which the white flare had been fired.

The jungle closed around them, a monstrous cloak of dark, heavy air. They drove on for almost two miles before grinding to a halt. A roadblock consisting of a jeep and a Citroen sedan blocked their path. Just off to the side of the roadblock was a British Land-Rover.

The Saladin, with Beidemann and George inside, nearly hit Casey's half-track in the rear before the brakes held. Fitzhugh saw the brighter glow of the truck's brake lights and brought his half-track to a quieter, more controlled stop.

The small convoy waited, engines idling. Beidemann let himself slide out the door of his armored car, taking his G-3 with him. From the rear of Casey's half-track, Yousef did the same, following in the big German's wake as he slipped into the shadowed darkness of the trees.

Casey stepped out. Only his half-track kept its lights on. They allowed him to see several figures move up to the roadblock. One stepped forward, a tall figure in leopard-type camouflage. The man smiled, his teeth very white in the lights from the half-track. With him were two others wearing the same kind of uniform, shiny new weapons carried at the ready. "Welcome, Mr. Romain, welcome. I am Colonel Lawrence Mtuba. My agents in the capital have radioed me that you were successful in your quest and the beast is dead. Congratulations. Please"—he indicated the shadows behind him with a sweep of his hand—"join us."

"Thank you, sir," Casey called out loudly. "Are the arrangements ready for our transport out?" Casey caught a glimpse of another figure standing in the darkness beyond the range of the half-track's lights. Something about the figure set him on edge. He kept on talking, his voice loud. "We want to get out of here as soon as possible. One of my men has a bad case of *bewacht*."

"Be . . . what, Mr. Romain? What is that?" queried Mbtuba.

Tensing, Casey repeated even more loudly than before, *"Bewacht."* There were enough men in his convoy who understood the German word. Casey had told them, "Beware! Something is not right up ahead." Van got ready to fire as the mortar crew stood by, shells on hand and ready to be dropped down the tube.

"That's a slang word used by my men for a gut wound," Casey told the confused ebony face in front of him.

"That is not a slang word. It's German and you are correct in being cautious, Mr. Romain. However, there is no real danger for you here that cannot be settled to everyone's satisfaction." The smooth voice came from the shadows near the Citroen, a voice that had the flavor of Asia, not Africa.

Not taking his eyes off the man in front of him, Casey greeted the unseen voice. *"Ni how ma?* You're a long way from home, Chinaman."

The lilting voice laughed gently. "You are more perceptive than I would have thought. You know that I am Chinese. What else?"

"Just this," replied Casey. A downward movement of his hand caused the half-track's lights to instantly go out. The men in front of the half-track were blinded by the sudden darkness for a few seconds as Casey dropped and rolled back to one side of the half-track, then leaped over it into the back, crying out, "Ambush! All fire and get moving!"

The Saladin seemed to erupt in a crescendo of automatic fire as its weaponry joined in with that of Casey's half-track. Tracers searched through the darkness for bodies to penetrate.

Instinct had first made Casey suspicious. When he'd seen the uniforms, he knew definitely. The jackets and trousers could have been bought anywhere, but he knew that the hats the N.F.L.K. men were wearing were straight out of Communist China, and the AK-47s they carried were the kind that China exported only to foreign factions she was supporting. They were the more finely finished models that were of much better quality than those issued the regular Chinese Army. That and the body English of the figure near the French sedan gave them away.

Before the startled figures in front of the half-track regained their vision, Casey had hold of his MG-34. Before Yousef left to follow after Beidemann, he'd already jacked a round in the spout and had a full belt of fifty in the drum. Cutting loose with the LMG, he sprayed to the front as the men behind him blasted away on both sides of the road. The mercs in the other vehicles were doing the same, using the steel sides of their transport for shelter as ricochets from return fire sparked off the metal.

One of the black troops in front of the half-track had a knee shattered by a burst from the MG-34 and fell screaming across the road. Casey yelled at Harrison, "Go, you slow son of a bitch, go!" Harrison gunned the motor. The armored beast lurched forward, the treads rolling over the squirming body in the road, crushing him from the waist down. Like a giant hemostat, the tracks pinched off the nerves and blood vessels in the man. From his belt buckle down he felt nothing. The man was dead. It was just going to be a bit of time before he knew it.

George got the Saladin's 20mm working. The heavy slugs, designed for penetrating light armor, ripped through tree trunks to find their targets, hitting more with wood splinters than with steel. Casey's half-track rammed into the cars blocking the road, pushing them aside as if they were a child's toys. Behind him, the Saladin came close on his heels, followed by the truck. A bit further back, the last half-track, which by now had its 60mm mortar in operation, was lobbing shells right and left as fast as the bombs could be dropped down the tube.

Casey's vehicle broke clear of the ambush, rushed ahead about twenty yards, then locked one track and spun around to face the way it had come in order to give fire support to the other vehicles. The Saladin took a position on the opposite side of the road, the 20mm blasting gaps in the jungle wall. Between the two of them they were able to keep most of the fire away from the more vulnerable truck, which rolled on between them, the men in it firing from both sides, tossing grenades right and left.

The whine of a large shell going overhead to burst in the trees to the right of the road said that Van was on his way. The rear half-track was laying out a scythe of fire, tracers cutting through the darkness until they made contact with a tree or a body. There was no way to tell how many N.F.L.K. troops surrounded them, but Casey figured that for them to have enough balls to stage this ambush, they had to have at least two-to-one odds.

The mercs' countermove had happened so fast, the N.F.L.K. troops were caught with their pants down. From the time the first shot had been fired until Van's half-track raced past Casey and George, less than fifteen seconds had elapsed.

To the would-be ambushers, this was an outrage. They were supposed to have cut down the hated whites with no difficulty.

Van's half-track moved on past Casey and George's holding position for another two hundred yards. It halted and started lobbing 60mm mortar fire and more high explosive rounds from the recoilless rifle. One of the mortar shells, a white phosphorus, landed smack in the middle of the road where a group of six N.F.L.K. soldiers were firing after the mercs. The cries of men in pain could be heard over the firing of the weapons. Burning bits of phosphorus ate holes in the flesh of all it touched. Some pieces the size of silver dollars burned all the way through the hair, scalp, and skull of its victims until it reached the brain and cooked the organ inside its own shell.

They were clear! Casey gave the word for his half-track and the Saladin to pull out. Reforming their convoy, they were out of sight of an infuriated Colonel Mtuba, who was yelling for his Chinese advisor.

The son of a bitch thinks he's so smart, thought Mtuba. *It's all his fault this happened!*

In seconds the convoy lights were lost in the dense jungle as they made it around a curve in the road and put the pedal to the metal. The Saladin kept its small turret facing to the rear, keeping a steady stream of fire going until it too disappeared behind the line of trees and went full out.

Casey cursed his luck, wondering who had sold them out and why. And he was going to find the answers to those questions. Of that he was damned sure.

CHAPTER THIRTEEN

Casey had them push their vehicles as hard as they could for another hour. Even at that, they usually went no faster than a crawl. The dusty track they were on was not one of the two paved roads of which Kimshaka could boast; it was more like a goat trail. But they didn't have any choice, and it was heading in the right direction. The first full light of day found the mercs heading south, the capital of Kimshaka eighteen miles behind them. Going over his alternatives, Casey knew that they'd have to get out of the country some way other than the one they'd planned on. He knew the location of the alternate pickup sites, but to get there with the N.F.L.K. this close to them would be impossible. And, he thought, if *he* were the rebel commander, he would have already called off the pickup, claiming the mercs never showed or were killed in action. It was time to review their options.

Behind him, he knew that Mtuba or someone like him would most probably be on their trail. But he had to stop and get his bearings before they went too far off-course and ran out of fuel. He called a halt on the far side of a narrow wooden bridge straddling about fifteen yards of a steeply banked, dry stream bed. From there they'd have a clear field of fire should the rebels come at them while they were resting. Before he had a chance to settle down, Beidemann approached, grinning broadly.

"Here's a souvenir for you." Beidemann's grappling hook of a hand forced a Chinese officer he had captured to his knees. "When me and Ali hit the brush during the ambush, we found him hiding behind a tree. He gave us no trouble at all, and I thought you'd probably like to talk to him when you had a chance."

"Good. I'd like very much to know who sold us out and why. But right now I don't have time for him. Put him in the truck with the wounded and keep him tied. Tell whoever you put on guard that if he causes any trouble, shoot him in the legs first. If he still acts up, tell him to do whatever he has to do to keep him quiet."

Beidemann turned his captive over to a South African merc, giving him Casey's instructions. Taking the Chinese man by the shoulder, he yanked him back up to his feet and aimed him in the direction of the truck with a firm boot in the butt. The merc wanted to be certain that the officer would do exactly as he was ordered without any hesitation.

After the Chinese officer was taken away, Casey gave

his commanders their orders. Fitzhugh and Beidemann put the men into position, telling them to chow down now as it might be a long time before they had another chance to do so.

From the side pocket of his camouflage trousers, Casey removed his survival kit which contained emergency rations of dried soup and high-potency vitamins, a tiny flare gun, a flexible saw, a fishing line and hooks, and a folded map of the area and neighboring countries. He tried to estimate their distance from the capital and at just what angle they were from it. The trail had headed mostly south, but there had been several long curves that could have taken them as much as six miles from where he thought they should be.

Once the men were out of the truck and armored vehicles, Fitzhugh set up a rear guard with the mortar and the 57mm to watch the way they had come. The others did the things they had to: taking a leak or crap, stretching their legs, digging into packs for something to chew on. The medic worked on the wounded, doing what he could with what he had. Van and George moved out, one on each side of the road, going on ahead to get a look at what was in front of them and to see if they could spot any landmarks.

Holding the map in his lap, Casey knew they were in a world of shit and that it was very likely that few, if any of them, would make it back to the airstrip they had so recently left. To the west was Angola, filled with Cuban soldiers; Tanzania, to the east, was not much better. There was no way they could head north without going right back into the arms of the N.F.L.K. By a process of elimination he decided they'd have to keep going south. If they weren't able to get to the airfield,

then they'd have to cross Barotseland until they reached
the Zambezi River. Once there, he'd have to make another choice: should they follow the Zambezi east to
Victoria Falls and try to get across to Rhodesia, or should
they cross the river at Sesheke on the Caprivi Strip? It
was the only place he knew of where they'd be able to
get their caravan across by ferry. Then they'd have no
choice except to just keep going south into the wasteland
of the Kalahari Desert until they reached the South African border. That was not a thought to bring one comfort.

Coming over and squatting down beside him, Harrison
brought up another option. He stroked his trim mustache
with what was probably the only clean pair of hands in
the group and said, "Look, Casey, if you can get us to
an airfield of any kind, I can get us out of here and save
a lot of wear and tear on our arses in the process." He
rubbed his butt to illustrate the discomfort of the armored
car's hard canvas seats. "Besides that, we don't have a
hell of a lot of petrol left for these fuel-guzzlers. If we
don't get some more, I'd guess we won't do more than
another fifty miles before they run dry. I really believe
that that would be the best approach to the matter."

Casey grunted. "That's true, and I'm in agreement.
Now"—he showed Harrison his map—"just where do
you think we'll be able to get a plane without getting a
bunch of our people killed first? By now the word is out,
and every strip that we know for certain would have
planes on it within a hundred miles of here will be armed
to the teeth with people who would love to have our guts
on a string. However, if we *are* lucky enough to find a
plane anywhere along the way, you'll certainly be the
first to know. Okay?"

Harrison walked off mumbling to himself about the
"bloody, smart-mouthed son of a bitch."

Fitzhugh climbed on top of the truck with a set of binoculars to watch in the direction from which they had come. Casey saw him and nodded approvingly. He was finishing off a smoke, waiting for Van and George to return, when Fitzhugh called down to him, "Dust over the trees about ten minutes away!"

Instantly the mercs went into defensive profiles as they waited for Casey's orders. Should they run for it or fight? The answer was obvious. There was no way of telling what they'd run into up ahead. Here, with the steep banks of the river bed and narrow bridge, they'd have the best chance to slow down their pursuers.

A shadow said that Van and George had returned.

"What's it like up ahead?"

Van shook his head. "Not so good. A couple of hundred meters on, the ground is open as far as the eye can see. Just low hills and brush."

That did it. If the N.F.L.K. were in any strength and caught up with them on open ground, they'd be dog meat. It was time to get things organized. Casey told one of the mercs to take Fitzhugh's place on top of the truck. "Fitzhugh, take some of the mortar rounds and set them to blow the bridge. Van, take over the fifty-seven, load it with high explosive, and when they get on the bridge, take out the lead vehicle but give Fitzhugh a few seconds' warning so he can time his charges. Gus, you take four men and cover the left flank. George, you do the same on the right. Use my thirty-four." Van, Beidemann, and George trotted off, picking up men as they went to set up their fire zones.

Fitzhugh took four of their precious few mortar shells and a hand grenade for each, and headed for the bridge. In only a few minutes he had each of the shells rigged with a grenade to serve as a detonator and placed where

it would blast through a supporting strut of the bridge.
The pins on the grenades had been straightened out. It
would take only a light tug at the lines attached to their
rings to pull them out. Fitzhugh ran the lines back to
where he had some cover behind a clump of sun-baked
boulders near the edge of the riverbank.

The dust clouds of the approaching vehicles could
now be seen by everyone. Casey told the merc on top
of the truck to come down; they didn't need him up there
anymore. The man scuttled over to join two of his comrades in a hastily dug foxhole.

All their vehicles had been moved out of sight behind
a small rise where they'd be easy to reach. The badly
wounded went with them to be out of harm's way.

From around the bend the sound of motors reached
them. Trucks in low gear were navigating around potholes big enough to crack their axles if they hit one hard
enough.

Now they had to wait out the next few minutes until
the enemy came into view. As always, the minutes
stretched into hours. Beads of perspiration gathered on
Casey's forehead, then followed the paths of least resistance down his face and cheeks, cutting clean channels
through the coating of reddish dust. He licked his lips
to moisten them, and waited.

"Here they come!" Casey barked.

The lead truck's motor changed sounds, shifting into
a higher gear as it reached the clear path leading to the
flimsy bridge.

Good, Casey thought. *They're too anxious. They've
already forgotten that sometimes one's prey will turn and
fight when least expected.*

• • •

Mtuba was in a rage. It had taken him nearly an hour to get the pursuit organized and to add four more trucks filled with additional men and arms from a nearby encampment to his now somewhat depleted force. At any rate, he had the foreigners outnumbered by about three to one with his two hundred freedom fighters. The six trucks and his own Land-Rover made up his command, one which he desperately desired to retain.

He had to catch them, or the best he could hope for would be to be put in front of a firing squad for losing the Chinese major. The mercenaries hadn't really mattered that much. It was just not considered prudent to have men of such expertise running around who could be used against them in Africa while they were taking over. But the presence of the Chinese advisor to the N.F.L.K. was a most carefully guarded secret. Even though units of the Front were already seizing power throughout the country in the wake of the vacuum created by Dzhombe's death, it was not too late for foreign interests to interfere if outsiders knew that the Chinese were supporting the N.F.L.K. and that the insurgents had no intention of living up to their agreements with the white contractors. *Damn Major Xaun for his arrogance!* He had insisted on being present at the ambush. His conceit could lead to the ruin of several years of painstaking, cautious negotiations. Everything had been kept highly secret. Now, when they almost had all they needed in their grasp, the fool screws things up and the foreign mercs had him. The Chinese were said to be a hardy race, but Mtuba had the feeling that the men who broke through his ambush would know how to get every last iota of information out of Major Xaun. If that happened before they were ready, all their plans would be ruined. There would be no highly trained battalions of North

Korean volunteers to offset the influence of the Cubans sent into Angola by the Russians. Nor would there be massive shipments of modern arms and equipment to enable them to subdue their neighbors, add strength to their own forces, and once and for all remove all signs of the white pestilence from the African continent.

Mtuba nearly cracked his head against the windshield of his Land-Rover as the driver suddenly swerved and hit the brake to avoid a pothole. He slapped the man across the side of the face, then looked ahead to the flat country where he would at last catch up to his quarry and either retrieve Major Xaun or kill him to prevent him from talking. He hit the driver again, urging him to use greater caution and faster speed.

Fitzhugh signaled with a jerky up-and-down movement of his arm. The first of the enemy trucks was in sight. Without seeing them, Casey could feel the tenseness of his men, ready and expectant. He nodded to Fitzhugh. He would let him use his own judgment as to when to pull the pins of the grenades and detonate the mortar shells. Everyone hunkered down even further, out of sight.

The lead truck picked up speed as it neared the bridge. Before crossing the bridge, the truck, a British Leyland, shifted down, then began to ease its weight across the structure. The second truck started across the bridge while the Leyland was still ten yards from the side where the mercs sat in ambush. Mtuba was in his Land-Rover between the third and fourth trucks.

They had gone far enough. Van signaled Fitzhugh, adjusted the sight on the 57mm resting on his shoulder, and fired.

The front of the Leyland burst into flame as the high explosive round from the 57mm smashed into it, killing the driver and the man riding shotgun. Before the explosion reached its peak, the mercenaries cut loose on the rear truck, blowing the tires to stop any retreat. Fitzhugh had timed the speed of the lead truck and pulled the cords to the grenade detonators five seconds earlier. While not as effective as detonator cord and C-4, the combined blast effect of the 60mm mortar shells cut the supports out from under the bridge, dropping the two trucks into the dry gully. The screams of the N.F.L.K. troops merged with that of the machine gun and automatic rifle fire from the mercs who were taking advantage of the "fish in a barrel" situation.

Mtuba's Land-Rover swerved to the side into a clump of brush. Behind and in front of him, his four remaining trucks screeched to a halt as their cargo of men unloaded and raced for cover.

Casey's mercs rushed to the edge of the riverbank, pouring every round they could into the trucks, cutting down anything that moved. Back and forth, they raked the river bottom. Most of the nearly one hundred and sixty men in the ambushed trucks had not been able to get out of them and were badly hurt when they hit the riverbed. It made no difference; wounded or whole, they all got the same treatment. Several hand grenades finished the action, exploding the gas in the trucks' tanks. Three men ran from the burning vehicles, their bodies covered in oily flames. Casey knew what fire like that felt like. To end their pain, he gave the word for them to be shot down.

Several rapid bursts of fire and the bodies lay still on the floor of the river with arms extended, hands clenched, legs drawn up under them, lips seared away to reveal grinning white teeth in charred faces. As they lay smoldering, the thick, sweet odor of human flesh cooking overrode that of cordite.

Mtuba screamed at his men to return fire. Several of Van's recoilless rifle rounds had landed too close. Firing a burst across the river from an AK-47, Mtuba smiled at the targets across the blown bridge. This time he was ready for them. They had no surprises left. He knew they had a 57mm, but he had something better and experts who knew how to use it for maximum effectiveness. The last truck backed up out of range and sight of the 57mm. From its rear, a long, lethal tube was withdrawn by its crew, taken to a small hill, and set up on its tripod. A round was loaded. The gunner sighted, and a 106mm shell flew across the riverbed.

Fitzhugh was just getting to his feet when the shell from Mtuba's recoilless rifle hit the ground between his legs. Fitzhugh's body was ripped to pieces. Lumps of flesh and bits of camouflage uniform were scattered for twenty yards in all directions. His head landed down in the river bottom by the corpse of one of the N.F.L.K. troops who had been burned. His white face and open eyes stared into the empty sockets of the African.

Five more of Casey's men were downed by Mtuba's gunners, their bodies shredded by shrapnel. On both flanks of the river, Mtuba's infantry were starting to lay down heavy fire. A platoon of rebels ran downriver to find a crossing that wasn't under the sights of the mercs.

Calling out as loudly as he could, Casey gave the word to bug out. "Run, you sons of bitches! Don't worry about covering fire! Just get out and to the trucks before we get our tails blown off!"

Another 106 screamed overhead. The heavy *crump* of its explosion was followed by the screams of wounded and dying men. Casey stopped to see what could be done. Only one out of the three was alive, his abdomen ripped open from sternum to groin, torn intestines strung out behind him like bloody ribbons. There was nothing to do for him but end his pain. One quick burst from his rifle put an end to the man's agony.

"Go! Go! Go!" he screamed at a group of stragglers who were trying to lay down covering fire. "I told you not to waste time with that! Get your asses on the trucks or be left behind!" They obeyed. With the enemy having the range on them with the 106 and outnumbering them in manpower, it was only a matter of time before they were flanked or totally blown to bits by the 106.

Once they loaded up, they gunned the motors and headed south. When the mercs had run for their vehicles, Colonel Mtuba ordered his gunners to raise their sights and go for maximum range, aiming in the general direction he knew the road would take. The convoy was nearly at the limit of the 106's range, when a round landed on the back of the rear half-track. Only the driver survived. The men in the rear of the half-track weren't recognizable as anything remotely human, yet the driver didn't have a mark on him. The Saladin whipped around to pick him up and was on the road again in less than fifteen seconds. George and Yousef had been riding in the destroyed half-track. . . .

Contact was broken, at least for the time being. Casey was furious with himself for taking the time to finish off the burning N.F.L.K. troops. Those few seconds gave the enemy time to get their recoilless rifle into position to fire. He should have broken contact immediately once

the bridge was blown. Now he had lost good men because
he wanted to spare the enemy pain. Not a good trade at
all, even though he knew that most of his men would
have given the same order. There was something horribly
sickening about being burned alive that went beyond
mere combat and the killing of one's foes.

The smoke of the stricken half-track rose over the hill
separating the mercs from Mtuba's view, but he knew
he had drawn blood again. Soon he would have the rest
of them. Now he had to take his remaining vehicles six
miles to the south where there was a crossing. He had
no doubt that he would catch up to them. It was only a
matter of time before he had them and the stupid Chinese
in his hands.

Van Janich asked Major Montfort, "Do we have any
more word as to the disposition of Mr. Romain's unit?"
Montfort had a worried expression on his face as he
answered the question. "No, sir. And I'll tell you this:
I don't like it. We know that Dzhombe is dead. That
much we have managed to confirm through our own
sources. And that is about all we can get. The N.F.L.K.
have only said that Mr. Romain and his men did not
make it to any of the rendezvous points. Since that time,
they have not responded to our attempts to communicate
with them."

Van Janich rubbed at his chin and its two-day stubble.
He had been at his headquarters since the day before the
mercenaries took off and had had Major Montfort report
back to him in person as soon as they'd departed.

"You are right, Major. Something is most definitely
wrong. I would not put it past our 'friends' in Kimshaka

to pull a double cross if they thought they could get away with it. But why? They need us to keep them in supplies and support until they secure power. The only way it would make sense for them to renege on our bargain is if they had a more powerful sponsor on their side. I do believe we should start looking more closely into the matter. There have been rumors of Oriental gentlemen being seen in the area."

Montfort nodded his head in agreement and dismissed himself to start things rolling. He had to know where the mercenaries were and why the N.F.L.K. were not responding to his calls.

CHAPTER FOURTEEN

Casey had to keep the pressure on, pushing the remaining half-track, the Saladin armored car, and the truck as fast as they could go. He had wanted to stop for the wounded but knew that if he did, Mtuba would be on them fast. He had to keep going in spite of the pain he knew it was causing some of the men. He had no choice. If they halted, they'd die. It was as simple as that. The only stops they made were to refuel from their nearly depleted stock of reserve gas carried in jerry cans. They had found a few gallons of gasoline in one of the villages and requisitioned it despite the protests of the Bombay-born Indian who'd said it was all the gas he had for his pride and joy, a 1949 Chevy station wagon without doors or fenders. They would have taken that, too, but Harrison had said that the way they were going, the old heap wouldn't last more than a few hours. Even with the Indian's reluctant contribution, there would be just enough fuel for one more refueling for the three vehicles, and that would be it unless they got lucky.

Traffic was nearly nonexistent. Word of Dzhombe's death and the fighting in the capital had somehow reached the area, most likely by radios at the trading posts.

It was almost sundown before they came to another halt. The land had given way to even sparser vegetation. Twice they had seen prides of lions sunning themselves lazily, unconcerned with the passage of the two war machines and the truck. Game was becoming more prevalent. Giraffes nibbled on tree branches as eland and gazelle grazed on knee-high yellow grass among small herds of wildebeest who stuck their tails in the air and trotted off, putting a healthy distance between themselves and the intruders.

They rattled through several small villages where natives, sitting with thin blankets wrapped around them in the shade of wattle and daub huts roofed with cone-shaped thatch or the rare, tin-roofed trading post run by an industrious Indian, watched them impassively. It was tempting to stop for a moment at one of the meat stands where goat meat and chickens hung from hooks, aging rapidly in the dry heat as clouds of iridescent blue and green flies swarmed over them.

The natives, who were not members of Dzhombe's ruling tribe, knew when to mind their own business. They just sat where they were, ignoring the clouds of dust thrown up by the mercs. This was none of their concern, and white men with weapons meant nothing good. It was best to leave them alone, unless one was either stupid or had a death wish. Besides that, it was too hot.

At a water hole on the south side of one of those dry, dusty kraals, the mercs stopped to rest and treat their wounded. They'd been lucky. None of the hit had received gut or head wounds, and the medic was able to treat them with penicillin and sulfa drugs to prevent infection.

The surviving mercs didn't blame Casey. He'd done the right thing. And there were at least forty to fifty rebels who wouldn't be on their trail anymore. Their own losses, including those killed at the bridge, stood at a total of eleven killed and five wounded, but the wounded were still able to fight.

Rinsing his face with water from a leather bucket, Casey stood by a well dug five years before by eager, young do-gooders from some American agency with a social conscience.

Beidemann walked slowly toward him, hands dangling at his sides as if he didn't know what to do with them. Casey felt a knot form in his stomach.

"What is it, Gus?"

"My old friend, I don't know just how to say this . . ." He let the words trail off awkwardly.

Casey knew Beidemann was bringing bad news, and it could only be one thing: one of his friends had been killed. Nothing else could have caused such a look of deep grief on the face of one such as the old German. The only question was . . . who?

"Go ahead, Gus. It's okay. Tell me who it is."

Beidemann was about to answer when Van called out from the turret of the Saladin.

"Casey, where's George?"

Casey felt both relieved and guilty at the same time. He was glad it wasn't Van and wishing it wasn't George. There was no way he could have chosen between the two of them. They were totally different men, but he loved them equally for many of the same reasons.

"He was in the rear half-track. Only the driver got out alive," Beidemann blurted out.

Van's smooth face began to crack as tears started to run down his cheeks.

"I was the one who picked up the driver. There wasn't enough left of those in the back to tell who they were." Beidemann paused. "Yousef was with them too," the big man said softly, as if by adding his own loss to the tally he could ease all of their pain a bit.

Casey blinked back his own tears. He had seen more men die than he cared to think about, but this hurt was as fresh as if he had lost the brother he'd never had. It took a great effort to bring his feelings under control. There was no time for mourning. He still had others in his charge who depended on him to see that they got out of this mess alive. He'd let his sorrow out later, when he was alone. And his surviving friends would deal with the losses in their own ways.

Beidemann was a realist about death. He, like Casey, had seen it come to many, and they had shared losses before, during the monstrous battles on the Eastern Front in Russia. Next to Casey, Ali ben Yousef was the closest thing he had to a friend, and like Casey, he felt both guilt and relief. He didn't know what god or gods George had believed in and wished the wiry Montagnard well in whatever future life he might encounter. As for Yousef, he had died in battle against those that the Moslems called infidels, which encompassed everyone who wasn't a Moslem. That should gain him some merit in the eyes of Allah.

Casey called the roll. With the five walking wounded who could still fight, it gave him a total complement of thirty-four men, counting himself. The fight at the bridge had been very costly.

As near as he could tell, they were about thirty miles from Barotseland. If they got that far, then perhaps Mtuba would call a halt to the chase once he reached the border. But Casey wouldn't want to give odds on it. He had something the African wanted: the Chinese major.

He told the men to take a break and sent out a rear guard. The remaining men were to refill the canteens, making sure they used their purification tablets. Then they were to check over their personal equipment, including ammo, weapons, and survival rations. While this was being done he sent for the Chinese.

Major Xaun, advisor to the insurgent forces of the National Front for the Liberation of Kimshaka, knew he was in a lot of trouble. He had fought against the Americans in Korea when he was a young man and knew their code for the treatment of prisoners. But from the look of these hard-faced professionals, he knew that claiming the same kind of treatment prisoners of war were normally entitled to by the Geneva Convention would be an exercise in futility.

His heart froze in his chest when he was put in front of the commander of the mercenaries. Gray-blue eyes locked as solidly as crystals of ice onto his own. The muscles in the scar-faced man's jaws worked like pistons to control the anger inside. Xaun knew the man with the scarred face and thick neck was only a hair's breadth away from killing him to release the anger and pain he felt because of the loss of his men. With this one, there could be no stalling or claims of ignorance, no tricks, and no attempt at any kind of negotiations. If he didn't give the mercenary what he wanted, then he would die.

"Name?"

Xaun spat it out as if it had a bad taste. "Major Han Pao Xaun."

"What is your purpose here?" Casey wasted no words on the man. He had neither the patience nor the time.

"We have been sent here as representatives of the People's Republic of China to lend assistance to the valiant freedom fighters of the N.F.L.K. as an act of solidarity."

Casey wiped a hand across red, tired eyes. "Cut the party line bullshit and tell me what is going on in as few words as possible, or I'll turn you over to my men to play with."

Xaun saw the big German looking at him as if he were a piece of steak and suddenly found it very difficult to swallow. The story he related was brief and to the point. China was looking to expand her sphere of influence to offset that of Russia. In addition, she had a great need for certain strategic raw materials that Africa could supply: industrial diamonds, chromium, manganese, bauxite, copper, and uranium. All of these and many others were in short supply in Communist China. When he answered Casey's questions about why the mercs had been ambushed, Xaun explained that it would look good to the outside world if the N.F.L.K. eliminated them to prove there had been no collusion between the rebels and any other parties. It would be a firm demonstration of the new African regime's firm dedication to the principles of noninterference by outside forces. In other words, the mercenaries had been pawns in a power play that ruled out the contractors and eliminated them. It had happened before.

Casey turned Xaun back over to a guard, telling him to let the major eat and drink before tying him up again. He had other things to attend to now. Calling Van to him, he had the Vietnamese take three men and go to the nearby village to scrounge up what they could in the way of food and gasoline, then he went to check on his wounded.

Spotting Beidemann by the half-track, he pulled him over to the side. "Gus, we're running low on fuel, and the half-track is slowing us down. I want you to drain whatever remains in its tanks and fill up the jerry cans. Then destroy the damned thing; I don't want Mtuba to be able to make use of it. Redistribute the cans between the truck and the Saladin. If you have to, have some of the men take turns riding on the outside of the armored car."

Next, he found Harrison trying to sleep, his head against the front tire of the Saladin. His normally dapper appearance was a disaster; sweat stains ran down his shirt, front and back, dust clogged every pore of his exposed flesh, and he needed a shave. Casey gave him a gentle nudge with the toe of his boot. "Get up, Harrison. There's work to do. And you can't do it if you're on your butt snoring."

Harrison turned a wounded expression on his leader. "My God, man, don't you have any consideration for me at all? I know the rest of you are savages and used to this kind of thing, but I'm a gentleman and a pilot, accustomed to a slightly higher, more refined standard

of living. Can't you see I'm a bloody wreck? I need a
bath, a shave, a drink of decent whiskey, and a good
lay, not necessarily in that order, mind you."

In spite of himself, Casey grinned. It was good to see
that some things never changed. When Harrison lost his
ascerbic wit, he knew they were all in deep trouble.

"Get up—we've got things to do. I want you to take
an ammo count and have it redistributed evenly among
the men. Don't take any crap from them. Just see that
they do it, then check over the Saladin and the truck. If
anything needs fixing, you have half an hour to do it.
Don't bother with the half-track; we're leaving it behind." Not waiting for any response, Casey headed for
the village, taking one of the South African mercs with
him to serve as an interpreter. He passed Van and his
party returning with three roasted goats and a dozen
chickens. The birds were being gnawed at on the way,
a trail of bones marking the men's path. He waved them
on toward the others, shouting to Beidemann, "Make
sure everyone gets some, or I may have to have your
well-larded ass barbecued as well." That brought a gale
of laughter from the waiting mercs who quickly lapsed
into an awkward silence as Beidemann glowered at them.

As Casey and his interpreter neared the line of mud
huts, mothers hustled their children inside to keep them
away from the eyes of the pale strangers. They had seen
whites before, those who came to dig wells and plant
crops that couldn't grow. The first were harmless if ignorant, but the others were like these hard-faced ones
who carried weapons and had the look of death about
them. One old man did not move. He sat in the shade
of his hut, brushing away the more persistent of the
swarming flies with a short whisk made from the tail

hairs of a wildebeest. His thin shoulders and knees were covered by a homespun, faded, red cotton mantle nearly as old as he was.

Casey told the South African what he wanted to know and stood behind him as the merc hunkered down on his haunches to be on eye level with the ancient black African. It took a couple of minutes before the two found a common tongue. Then, after a series of clucking sounds, eye movements, and many hand and arm gestures from the old man, the merc finally stood up, politely thanked the old one, and turned back to Casey.

"The old guy says there is nothing ahead of us for at least a three-day walk. There are a few guards at the border of Barotseland, but he says they do nothing but drink thin beer and sleep. He does know that not too far across the border there is an airstrip used by a Dutch mining franchise to bring in supplies and men. One of his sons works for them."

At that, Casey perked up. A private field across the border in Barotseland would probably not be well guarded, and it was also quite possible the Dutchmen knew nothing of their approach. If that were the case, then he might be able to get Harrison his plane after all. From his pocket he tossed the old man a pack of cigarettes in thanks for his help. After their backs were turned, the old one threw the pack across the dirt street and spat at the tracks of the whites.

By the time Casey got back, the half-track had been disabled by Harrison's skillful hands. Its tanks were drained of the few gallons of gasoline remaining in them, and the men who had been in it were assigned to their new positions. It would be a bit crowded in the two remaining vehicles, but it couldn't be helped. The Saladin was designed for a crew of four. Now it carried twelve, most of them hanging onto the outside. The remaining men and all their heavy weapons were in the truck. The mortars, recoilless rifle, and ammo took up nearly all the floor space. If anyone was going to sleep, he'd have to do it sitting up on the wood benches or on top of the weapons.

Calling his men together, Casey briefed them on their situation.

"Men, we were sold out. Not by the contractors, but— as you've probably guessed—by the N.F.L.K. The situation is this: To the south and east is Rhodesia, but I think that option is too risky for us to try right now. The roads are probably being watched, and the border patrols will have been alerted. So we are going to keep heading south a bit longer to Barotseland. After we get across the border, I have been told there may be an airstrip run by some Dutchmen not too far from there. If we're lucky, we might be able to liberate a plane and get out of here by tomorrow. If not, then we try a straight run east for Rhodesia. If for any reason we get separated from each other, don't waste time looking. Just head for the Victoria Falls crossing on the Zambezi River and turn yourself over to the Rhodesians. If anyone tries to stop you, do what you have to. Once in Rhodesia, they'll help you get out of the country. I'm putting Gus in command of the truck. I'll keep the Chinese with me, but he is to be turned over to the first white troops we meet. If anything happens to me, he can help pay back the N.F.L.K. for us. Now load up and keep your eyes open. Let's go!"

CHAPTER FIFTEEN

Mtuba was in a lather. His last radio communication with headquarters had made it crystal clear that his head was on the line. They were not able to send him any additional support. All N.F.L.K. manpower was committed to the fighting now taking place with Dzhombe's followers, who were offering fierce resistance at several barracks and strong points. The revolution had no men or equipment to spare. The problem had to be solved by him and the men he had with him. If he did not recover Major Xaun, there'd be hell to pay—and he'd be the one doing the paying.

He'd lost even more time when one of his trucks hit

a patch of soft sand and had to be dug out. It was entirely possible that the mercenaries would reach the border of Barotseland before he caught up. Then what would he do? Thanks to the gods, the old half-track had kept the mercenaries' speed down to a minimum or they would already be out of his range. From the people of the villages he'd passed, he'd learned he was closing the gap. Though most of the ignorant beasts couldn't tell time, they still made it clear he was gaining. But was he doing it fast enough? When he found the abandoned and ruined half-track, he was able to get a count on their strength. He still had the right numbers on his side, and the mercenaries were down to two vehicles. And not much fuel was to be had on the route they were taking. It was also possible that the guards at the Barotseland border might turn them back, or they might just go around the checkpoint. That's what he would do in their case.

With the Saladin in the lead, the mercs rolled south all that day and through the night, passing sleeping villages whose only signs of life were the glow of campfires and the yapping of dogs. On the Saladin, the men hanging onto the outside traded places with those confined to the cramped interior. There they could at least close their eyes and not have to worry about falling off. In the jolting two-and-a-half-ton truck, men sat with weapons between their legs or across their laps on the hard wooden benches. Others tried to find places on top of the heavy weapons and ammo. Twisting their bodies around, leaning against each other for support, they tried to sleep, eyes snapping open at every bump in the road or the distant, chuckling hysteria of a hyena who had found the carcass of some animal to feed on.

In the blue haze of the night moon, termite hills stood as lonely outposts in the distance. Some were over fifty years old, older than most of the independent black African nations on the continent. Headlights searched out the road in front. Behind, clouds of dust were twisted and swirled by the warm evening breezes until the dry soil settled back onto the land. When the rains came, the sun-baked road would become a cloying, sucking mass that no vehicle without deep treads could ever hope to traverse. It was an empty place for modern man, yet there were things under the thin soil that nations would go to war over. Fantastic wealth waited for those lucky or stubborn enough to beat the land and force out of it the dreams most of them died for without ever seeing.

Casey wearily watched the beams of light in front of him as the miles rolled past. His eyes ached from the grit of the road and from lack of sleep. They stopped briefly when they met an aged Volkswagen and had left its owner screaming at them in impotent fury as they drained his tiny car of the few gallons of gas in its tanks. They stopped twice more so that the drivers could be changed. Casey would have no accidents because of exhausted men. Whenever they reached a rise, he'd twist around in the turret and look behind him, hoping he'd see no lights.

To him the land seemed especially empty. He had been there long ago, when the great herds of elephant, gazelle, wildebeest, and zebra had moved in huge waves that took days from the time the first one crossed a mark until the last straggler went by. There were still animals out there, but like the land, they had been overused: poached, harvested, or driven out by the herds of cattle and goats the natives needed to feed their own growing

populations. And with the domesticated herds came over-
grazing, until each year the desert claimed a few more
miles of land, turning it into a haven for snakes and
scorpions, leaving less ground fit for the use of either
man or animal.

An hour before dawn he called another halt. From a
rise in the road he saw the flicker of distant light: the
frontier and Barotseland. A few shacks and a single plank
hut were the only structures to show that they were entering a different country. He ordered the lights turned
off on the truck and the Saladin. By the light of the stars,
they turned to the east to bypass the outpost. They'd
cross the border farther down, then swing back. There
was little likelihood they would have any trouble from
anyone they met. Even his few men were more than a
match for any of the scarce, ill-equipped, poorly trained
local troops they might run into. And if they were spotted,
it was more than likely they would simply be ignored.
The Africans often looked at things that way. Sometimes
not seeing something made life that much easier.

Mtuba lowered the binoculars from his eyes. He was
pleased that he had ordered his men to turn off their
lights a half hour earlier. With the aid of the glasses he
had seen the two-and-a-half-ton truck's taillights go out
as it turned off the road. He would have them by dawn.

The lone sentry on duty at the border station thought
he heard the sound of motors for a moment, but he
shrugged his shoulders as the sound faded into the distance.

* * *

They were across the border. Not until they had driven another three or four slow, torturous miles in the darkness did they turn their lights back on. Breaking trail through the brush, the Saladin nearly ran over a tent in a dry wash. Both vehicles came to a thumping, bone-jarring halt. From inside the tent came a volley of curses that would have done even Beidemann proud.

"What the bloody, fucking hell do you goddamned idiots think you're doing driving around the bleedin' bush like some ignorant, fucking Kaffirs out on a lark?"

His protests ceased abruptly when the muzzle of Casey's automatic looked down at him from the turret of the armored car. Clearing his throat, he changed his tone and introduced himself as John Grimes, an itinerant and luckless prospector. "Well, then, I guess you do have the right to drive wherever you want to."

Casey climbed down from the turret, jumping off the fender to stand in front of the grizzled, scruffy man in faded khakis and bush hat. "Take it easy, old-timer," he said. "We're not going to hurt you unless you do something foolish."

Grimes, or Grimy as he claimed his friends called him, scratched at a week-old gray stubble with a dirty fingernail as he sized up what he saw. Armed white men in a black country. "Well, now, I don't believe I'm that far around the bend to argue with a bloody bunch of mercenaries with machine guns in their hands just because they nearly ran me over in the privacy of my own home." He indicated the worn, patched, one-time British Eighth Army field medical tent. He bobbed his head up and down as if agreeing with himself. "I know who you blokes are. I caught it on my battery radio yesterday. You've got to be the ones who put the quits to that bloody

maniac, Dzhombe." He didn't wait for the scar-faced
man to agree with his deduction. "Well, then," he continued in more pleasant tones, "that puts a different light
on things. Welcome, and if there's anything I can do,
just ask old John Grimes, and if he's got it, it's yours."

Beidemann and Van joined Casey, who told them,
"Let the men get out and stretch their legs for a moment.
Our new friend and I are going to have a few words.
But keep an eye on Xaun. I don't want to lose him just
yet." Beidemann grunted an acknowledgment, then told
the others to off-load and do whatever they had to do.

Grimy watched the men in their camouflage fatigues
with amusement and interest. "It looks like you boys are
a bit the worse for wear. But what are you doing this far
south? I know enough about your line of work to know
you should have been long gone to wherever you came
from by now. Someone fucked things up, eh?" Whatever
else old Grimy might have been, he wasn't slow in the
thinking department.

Taking Grimy with him back to the truck, Casey un-
folded his map. By the dim light of the dash, he pointed
to what he figured was their approximate position. "Is
this where we are now?"

Grimy took a pair of bifocals from a metal case he
kept in his shirt pocket and put them on. Peering down
at the spot indicated, he nodded his head up and down.
"That's close enough, but where are you going? Rhodesia? If you are, then you're heading in the wrong direction. There's nothing to the south but hard country.
And if you get across the Zambezi into Botswana and
keep going south, all you'll find is the bleedin' Okovanggo swamps. Beyond that, there's nothing but that
godforsaken wasteland, the Kalahari. And I don't think

you're going to get much help from the locals getting there. They didn't like Dzhombe, but they hate white mercenaries even more."

Casey didn't argue with him or offer any explanation. "What I want to know is this: Is there a Dutch mining company around here with an airstrip?" he asked.

Grimy grinned, showing long, tobacco-stained teeth. "So that's it. You're going to try and fly out of here. Well, now, that's a good idea. I don't like those damned Dutchies much anyway. Several times they've run me off of what they say is their digs."

Casey was beginning to get a bit impatient with the old man's rambling. "Just answer the question. We don't have forever."

Grimy grunted, a bit offended. "All right, all right! Yes, there is a field, and they have an old Dakota there most of the time. You might be lucky and find it on the ground, but the Dutchies aren't going to like it, and they can be a bunch of mean bastards." He took a closer look at Casey's face. "I guess you people will be able to handle it all right. Here's where the strip is located." He put a black fingernail on a spot on the map near Kasempa. "It should take you about an hour to get there from here if you cut straight west for about five kilometers, then follow the road they built to their claim due south for another ten. The road's not on the map, but it's there all right. When you see a flat-topped kopje with termite hills on top of it, you'll know when to turn south. You'll run right into the road. You can't miss it."

Casey sighed with relief. The old prospector had finally gotten to the point. Turning off the dash light, he called for Beidemann.

"Tell Harrison we might have a plane for him. Get

everyone back on board, and let's get out of here." Before leaving, he asked Grimy, "Is there anything we can do for you?"

Grimy shook his head. "No, I got all I need right here. I'm just glad you put the shaft to old Dzhombe. It was long overdue."

Lights back on to make better time, they followed John Grimes's directions. The prospector was right on the money. Exactly where he said it was, they saw the flat-topped mound with the termite hills on it and turned south. To the east, the false dawn added enough light so they were able to turn off theirs. For all of them, the next minutes were filled with tension, anxiety, and a dread that there would be no plane at the Dutch strip. But if they were lucky, they would soon be safe.

Mtuba had no trouble following the tracks of the armored car and truck as he pressed hard to catch up. He nearly repeated what Casey had done, almost running over Grimy's tent. The old man responded even more testily than he had the first time. Mtuba could tell from the tracks on the ground and sand that the mercenaries had stopped here for some time. If so, there could only be one reason why; they had wanted to know something. Now he would find out what the filthy prospector had told them. It took him thirty precious minutes to learn where the mercenaries were heading and why. He hated to lose the time questioning the old man, but now he knew where to go.

They left John Grimes's body where it lay. The old man's fingers were ground under the tires of Mtuba's Land-Rover. The rest of him was several feet away. Before they left the gully, the scent of fresh blood had drifted on the dawn breeze, drawing jackals and hyenas toward their breakfast.

The Dutch mining road was in better shape than the state ones. It ran straight and smooth with a minimum of the spine-jerking potholes that waited for the unwary driver like snipers. With the sun, they came across signs posted along the road, warning in English, Dutch, French, and the local dialects that this was private property and trespassers would be punished.

The men were covered with dust. It coated the insides of their mouths, noses, and ears. Small clouds erupted from their uniforms when they hit a bump. Dust was what most of them would remember about their scenic tour of rural Kimshaka and Barotseland.

A glint of light from the tin roofs of several buildings in the distance brought them to one last stop. Standing on top of the turret of his armored car, Casey strained his eyes, slowly scanning from right to left. There it was! A brighter gleam on the right side of the buildings beckoned them like the No Vacancy sign on a cheap motel. The plane was there! They had a way out!

"Let's go, men! There's our bus!" From the truck came a half-hearted cheer from the tired men. Slowly the Saladin started off; it had less than two miles to go. Casey hoped he'd have no serious trouble with the owners of the plane. But at this point, there was more at stake with their reluctant passenger, Major Xaun, than with the Dutch mining concern. Looking back the way they'd come, Casey felt his stomach turn over. Coming over a long, low rise was the lead truck of the pursuing N.F.L.K. convoy. Behind it came Mtuba's Land-Rover. They were not out of the thick of it yet. If the plane wasn't fueled and ready to go, it was still very possible they'd all end up either dead or in a Kimshakan prison. They'd probably be better off dead.

Mtuba was elated. Now he'd take them all. He only hoped that the scar-faced leader of the mercenaries would be alive when he got his hands on him. He had plans for that man that did not include an easy death. He would kill him an inch at a time to make him pay for the inconvenience he had caused. Sticking his head out of his window, he yelled to the trucks behind the Land-Rover, ordering the men in them to get ready.

Montfort had the driver of his prized Bentley turn off on the road leading to van Janich's headquarters. He had received a report that was most disturbing. It was rumored that Communist Chinese troops were seen with the N.F.L.K. when they took Kimshaka City. Perhaps that had something to do with the disappearance of Casey Romain and his men. Something rotten was going on, and they were a long way from Denmark. He was curious to see what van Janich would make of this new information. Things could begin to get a bit sticky. He found it difficult to believe that the mercenaries could simply vanish without a trace. That was too much, really!

CHAPTER SIXTEEN

At the south end of the strip, the old Dakota sat by a makeshift hangar and workshop. The Saladin pulled over at the north end of the runway. As the truck pulled up alongside the armored vehicle, it stopped long enough to let five men and Beidemann bail out, taking the 57mm recoilless rifle with them to add support to the 20mm on the Saladin. The mortars went with Van and Harrison. They'd probably be needed to give the rear guard cover when they had to withdraw. After transferring Major Xaun to the truck, Casey kept only three men with him in the Saladin: a driver, a loader, and a machine gunner. The others joined the rest of the mercs near the truck, waiting for orders.

From the advantage given him by the height of the turret, Casey did a quick surveillance of the approach the rebels would have to take to reach them. Once off the road and in sight of the field, they'd be able to flank them. The terrain all around was open, broken only by brush and scrub trees, none more than ten feet tall. They needed to engage the enemy before they got this far.

"Gus, this is going to be tricky. We can't cover every approach, so we've got to draw them to us. I want you to take these men and head straight out. Take the fifty-seven with you. I want you to hit the first vehicle that comes into range. When you do, I'll have the Saladin on their left flank and start turning the line against them. Watch out for me. I don't want one of your shells up my tail. Maybe we can keep them busy until Harrison and Van get the plane secured. Keep your ears open. We'll probably have to back off in a hurry, one way or another."

Casey directed the Saladin to where they'd have the most cover from the trees. The 20mm gun was loaded; inside, belts of oiled machine gun ammo were made ready. As soon as Mtuba's men came into range, they'd fire and try to hold them off until they heard the sounds of the Dakota's engines turning; then they'd make a run for it.

Beidemann made for the brush. His men spread out in a thin skirmishing line, weapons at the ready, safeties off. He carried a G-3 rifle in one hand and the heavy recoilless rifle in the other. On his shoulder was a sack containing their last five rounds.

Xaun twisted his shoulders around, trying to ease the burning pain in them and his back. His bonds had made it nearly impossible for him to get any sleep. From what the mercenaries were saying, he knew that Mtuba was coming for him. Good, then he would have his revenge!

The truck screeched right up to the side of the plane. Men piled out of the back and threw a cordon around the aircraft. This was to be their salvation, their only way out. They'd let no one near it at any cost. Van took two men with him into the hangar. Inside were four men, one white and three black, who kept the plane and hangar in order. Their questions were stopped by the sight of automatic weapons pointing at them and the expressions on the mercs' faces. These were not men to argue with. Van waved them over to a screen-walled cage where tools were kept.

"Inside! No talking, no questions, and maybe you'll still be alive an hour from now. We don't want anything from you except the plane." The four men made no protests. They had been around long enough to know when to keep their mouths shut and obey orders. Van used the padlock that was on the cage—intended to keep thieves out of the tool room—to lock the mechanic and his helpers inside where they wouldn't get in the way. To the other men with him he barked, "Check out the rest of the building. If there's anyone else here, put them in the cage too."

A quick search turned up no one else. Leaving the mechanic and his helpers inside, they returned to the cordon around the plane. Harrison was already in the cockpit checking it out. Leaning his head out the cockpit window, he yelled down at Van, "We need gas." Pointing to a manual pump and some fifty-five-gallon drums near the hangar, he said, "Check those out and if there's anything in them, get a couple of men to pump it into the wing tanks."

"Right!" Van detailed five men to check out the drums and to begin rolling the full ones over to where they could be hooked up to the pump and lines. Another climbed onto the wings to open the caps over the tanks.

"How long will it take?" Van called up to Harrison.

The pilot snapped back, "Until I get enough in this son of a bitch to be sure we can get to Rhodesia. I'll let you know. Now get them moving so we can get the hell out of here!"

Van yelled up to him about the men he'd locked in the tool cage. "I think one of them's a mechanic. Do you want to talk to him?"

Harrison popped his head back out. "Bet your ass I do! If there's anything wrong with this antique, I want to know about it now rather than at ten thousand feet! I'll be right out."

Jumping out of the plane's side door, he followed Van inside the hangar. The mechanic did not like being locked up, and while not stupid enough to give them any back talk, he had suddenly gotten a bit stubborn and decided he wasn't going to tell them anything. Harrison got nothing from him other than dirty looks. He expressed his frustration to Van. "I can't get anything out of him one way or the other. If he did tell us anything, how would we know if he's telling the truth?"

Van thought that over for a moment, then grinned under his coating of dust. "That's easy. Tell him he's going up with us. That way, if anything goes wrong, he'll be right there when we go down."

"Good idea, you wily Oriental gentleman. Did you hear that, you obstinate Dutchman? If we go down, you'll go down with us." Jan Reiks turned a pale green. Chewing one fingernail with a ten-year undercoating of grease, he reevaluated his decision.

His English was good, though heavily accented. "Since you put it that way, there are a few things. The warning light is out on the hydraulics, and the line to the landing gear is disconnected."

Harrison told Van to take him out of the cage, then pointed a warning finger at Reiks. "All right, now you get out there and fix it and do it right, because you're still going up with us. One more thing—you don't have much time. There are some very angry people coming after us who want our guts for garters. They won't know you're not one of us, and they'll cut your bloody white head off as fast as they will ours."

Reiks swallowed, his Adam's apple sending signals. "It will take only five minutes." Running back into the cage, he brought out a tool chest and a five-gallon can of hydraulic fluid.

Mtuba moved his Land-Rover to the front, out from his safe place between the two trucks. Putting his field glasses back up to his eyes, he adjusted the focus. The plane came sharply into view. He could see men around the plane and on its wings. The truck was there, but where was the armored car?

The radiator on Mtuba's rear truck suddenly erupted in a spout of flame and steam. Casey's 20mm round had hit it squarely. Mtuba's men scrambled out of the truck, but they took their weapons with them, including the 106mm recoilless rifle. Casey whipped the Saladin in and out of the brush, his machine gunner raking over the trucks. They had to be put out of commission to give their men on the field time to get the plane working.

Mtuba's gun crew were pretty good. They had the 106 set up and loaded in less than a minute. The Saladin came out of a patch of brush, the 20mm and the machine gun firing. Three of Mtuba's men went down. The 106 fired, the shell hitting the Saladin right above the left front tire, blowing it and the fender off, and sending red-hot shell splinters inside the car to bounce off the steel sides. Casey was thrown out of the turret as the armored car turned over. Landing solidly on his back fifteen feet away, he was stunned. From inside the car, screams could be heard as the fuel tanks exploded, turning the interior into an iron furnace. Exploding ammunition brought a merciful end to the two mercenaries' agony.

Mtuba called to his men, pointing at the dazed Casey, "Get that man for me and knock out that plane! Without it they can't get anywhere!" Three men ran for Casey as the 106 crew manhandled their long tube around, readjusting the sight for their new target.

The men of the N.F.L.K. were nearly upon Casey, running, crouched low, weapons at their hips ready to fire. They were stopped by a strange whooshing noise that shredded their bodies, tearing holes through their chests, and ripping faces and skulls apart.

Beidemann came out of the bushes to the left of Casey. Behind him, the men on the 57mm reloaded with high explosive, having used their last round of canister on the three Africans. Beidemann yelled back at them, "Hit the enemy gun!"

Bending over Casey, Beidemann grabbed his friend's arm and jerked him to his feet. Throwing him over his shoulder, he ran back into the brush, bullets clipping at his feet. The mercs on the 57mm fired one round, missing the enemy recoilless rifle but scaring the shit out of Mtuba when the round passed close enough to his Land-Rover that he could have reached out and touched it.

• • •

Van looked across the field to where the fight between his friend and Mtuba was taking place. His men were setting up empty steel drums for cover. Jan Reiks worked as feverishly as the crew, who were refueling the plane's tanks under the frantic urging of Harrison. Reiks had reconnected the hydraulic lines to the landing gear, filled the reservoir with fluid, and had just finished bleeding the lines. Throwing the empty can over by the hangar, he called up to Harrison, "That's it!"

Checking his fuel gauges, Harrison yelled out to the men on the wing tanks: "Cap that son of a bitch off!" To Van, he waved his arm. "Get 'em on board!" Two mercs leaped through the open cargo door as Van prodded Xaun to his feet. Two more men grabbed the Chinese and threw him bodily up to the pair waiting for him. In relays they began to climb on board.

A round from Mtuba's 106 blasted three oil drums high into the air, killing one Belgian. Van was glad the drums were empty, or they would have sprayed the plane with burning oil and gasoline. Another shell hit on the dirt runway, shrapnel splinters splattering the fuselage, breaking out the right window on the copilot's side.

"What the bloody hell are you waiting for?" Harrison screamed at Van as he hit the starter switch and opened the throttle.

That was all the encouragement Van needed, and he followed the last of the men on board as the port engine coughed into life. By the time he'd run up to the cockpit, the starboard motor was running. Harrison wasted no time. As soon as he could, he started the plane rolling back down the runway to the north. He could have taken off to the south, but he wanted to get as close as possible to those who were fighting their rear-guard action. Seconds meant life, and he was not going to leave them behind just to save his own neck. From the open cargo door and along the windows that the mercs had smashed out, machine gun and automatic rifle muzzles stuck their lethal spouts out the sides of the cargo plane as firing apertures were made.

Running, twisting, and dodging through the brush and trees, Beidemann carried Casey toward the landing strip. The men on the 57mm fired off their last rounds and covered his retreat with light weapons fire, spraying the N.F.L.K. in front of them, trying to make them keep down until they could break free and follow after the big German.

Mtuba kept after the 106 crew to keep firing, cursing them for missing a target as big as the plane. Now the damned thing was moving! All his men were out and on their stomachs, firing wildly at everything that moved, including the breeze through the dry leaves of the brush.

"Cease fire, you fools! Wait until you have something to shoot at!" A burst of bullets from one of the rear-guard mercs shattered the Land-Rover's windshield.

"Why aren't you firing?" he screamed as he hit the ground, his face bleeding from glass splinters.

The two mercs caught up with Beidemann, who turned Casey over to them. They placed his arms around their shoulders and half carried, half dragged their semiconscious leader to the north end of the landing strip.

Beidemann broke to his right. Taking advantage of all the cover, he ran to get around the flank of the enemy. He had to get that 106 out of action before they hit the plane or damaged it so badly they couldn't take off. For all his bulk, Beidemann could move fast when he had to. Getting around the flank, he dropped to his stomach and went into a crab walk. His body raised half off the ground, his weapon on his chest, he scurried from bush to bush until he was behind them.

Under the lash of Mtuba's tongue—and the sincere threat of execution—the N.F.L.K. troops managed to get into a semblance of order. Getting them into a line, Mtuba ordered them to advance at a half run toward the end of the air strip. Overhead, the 106 sent another round arcing into the sky to blast a small pit twenty feet in front of the Dakota as Harrison zigged and zagged closer to where the two mercs with Casey waited for it to come and get them.

The crew operating the 106 concentrated their attention to the front as they tried to adjust to the changing distance and position of the Dakota on the strip. They never saw or heard the figure to their left raise up and draw the bolt back on his weapon. Thirty 7.62mm rounds ripped through their backs, tearing hearts and lungs open. The three men of the recoilless rifle crew died instantly. Another object fell through the air to fall among the bodies by the boxes containing the shells for the recoilless rifle.

Mtuba dropped to his knees and turned around when he heard the firing behind him. He just had time to see the grenade land among the shells and scream "Down!" before it went off. The explosion threw the 106 fifty feet away, its tube twisted and warped. A fireball rose overhead, and smoking white flakes began to fall to earth, many of them landing on several of his men, who immediately quit whatever they were doing and went into spasms, slapping themselves. They clawed at their uniforms, screaming as they tried to put out the burning pieces of white phosphorus eating their way deep into their flesh.

Beidemann gave the backs of the N.F.L.K. another full burst, then he dropped and rolled out of sight, going back the way he had come. He'd have to hurry; the Dakota was nearly at the end of the strip.

CHAPTER SEVENTEEN

Harrison worked the throttles, giving the old bird just enough juice to keep her under control. He tried to navigate to where he saw the two mercs with Casey. *But where the hell is Gus?* he wondered. Suddenly he heard a heavy explosion, and then he noticed that there were no more 106 rounds coming at them. That gave him his answer. "So, Gus got the sons of bitches! Bloody good!"

A round from an SKS assault rifle poked a hole through Beidemann's left leg, a neat, round puncture in the fleshy meat of his calf. But he didn't stop moving. The skirmish line of the N.F.L.K. was too near the end of the strip. They were advancing, firing from the hip. The two men with Casey were trying to hold them off, but there were too many. He needed to get back to them as fast as he could. He knew the wound was not too bad and figured the bullet that hit him had to be one of the military-issue slugs with a copper jacket. Soft lead or a dumdum would have knocked him down and torn up the leg.

As Harrison taxied the plane nearer to the two mercs with Casey, the men in the aircraft had their weapons angled as far out the windows as they could to provide firepower aimed at the advancing line of rebels in the trees. There wasn't much chance they'd hit too many, but perhaps it might slow up Mtuba's line a little.

Beidemann stumbled and fell. Before he could get to his feet, he was knocked back down. His left shoulder was smashed at the socket by another round fired from point-blank range. One of Mtuba's men, a member of the Luba tribe, was trying frantically to reduce the stoppage in his AK-47. The bolt was jammed with an expended cartridge casing that was half in and half out of the chamber, caught between the bolt and the chamber. Beidemann rose, and sweeping his good hand like a scythe, he knocked the legs out from under the Luba. Jerking the jammed rifle out of the man's hand, he swung it by the barrel, crushing the man's head.

Staggering back to his feet, he retrieved his own G-3 and looked to see if there was anyone within sight he could kill. Seeing nobody, he took off again, ignoring the burning dead weight of his useless left arm.

Casey was back on his feet, his head clearing from a crack that would have given a normal man a migraine for the rest of his life. Shaking the cobwebs from his brain, he took stock of the situation. The Dakota was almost to them. There was a shout from the left as Beidemann staggered out of the trees, a trail of blood marking his path. Bullets whipped around him.

Casey dropped to one knee, firing short, three-round bursts into the trees behind his wounded friend. A cry of pain gave him some satisfaction. Giving the two men with him cover, he sent them to get Beidemann. Grunting under their load, they obeyed Casey's instructions and stumbled out onto the strip.

The Dakota was beginning to make its turn so that it would face back down the runway. Shots from the N.F.L.K. poked holes through its sides. They buzzed erratically inside the cargo bay like angry bees, ricocheting until they fell to the deck. As the plane made its turn, the return fire from its windows increased as more guns could be brought to bear. Van had left the copilot's seat and had moved back inside. Setting up the 60mm mortar in the cargo door, he hand held it on the butt plate and began to lob rounds into the trees.

The N.F.L.K. were almost on them. Casey concentrated on every shot, making most of them count as the enemy grew visible in the brush. Moving from one spot to another, hiding behind trees or even tall clumps of grass, he held them off. Looking over his shoulder as he changed magazines, he saw the two mercs heave Beidemann up into the cargo bay with the help of waiting hands. The plane completed its turn, showing the enemy its tail. Van cried out over the roar of the engines for Casey to run, which he did, waving for Harrison to go ahead. Harrison gave it a bit more gas, and the bird started to taxi. Casey was almost to the cargo door when a round hit his left thigh. He fell, and the distance between him and the plane increased to thirty feet. Mtuba was on the north end of the strip, his men laying down all the fire they could muster at the retreating plane. If the plane stopped now, even for a few seconds, all would die. Casey staggered back to his feet. Calling upon hidden reserves of strength, he ran after the plane. In one last, final burst of energy, he grabbed hold of the guy lines on the tail and pulled himself up on the flat blades. Van had to be stopped from jumping out of the cargo bay and going to him.

Harrison leaned out as far as he could from his window and looked back. A bullet nearly took his ear off as machine gun fire raked the side of the plane. He could see Casey hanging onto the ailerons. He gave the old bird some more gas, increasing its speed; he still had some runway left. Inside, Beidemann was being treated by the medic, who was frantically trying to stop the bleeding from his nearly ripped-off arm. Harrison knew that he couldn't slow down too much or he'd never be able to get up the speed necessary to take off on what runway remained. And if he did take off, the first time he pulled back on the stick, he'd knock Casey off. He came up even with the hangar, and Casey made his decision for him and let go, rolling to the ground. He stood on his feet and waved for Harrison to go on, crying out, "There's nothing you can do! Get the hell out of here if you can!" Then he turned to fire back down the strip, hitting one more of Mtuba's men with a lucky shot.

Van was screaming in rage and fury at Casey's being left behind. It took three men to hold him back. One of them threw a G-3 and a pack containing ammo, grenades, and rations out the open cargo door, figuring that the longer reach of the rifle would give Casey a better chance. But no one inside the plane really believed he had any chance at all. Tears in his eyes, Harrison laid it on, pushing the throttle until the old plane vibrated from stem to stern as it picked up speed. The cargo door was closed just as the wheels lifted off at the end of the strip, barely clearing the line of trees. They were airborne and safe. Banking the bird to port, Harrison could see Casey. He'd reached the G-3 and the pack, and was heading for the hangar, laying out fire as he went.

Mtuba was in a rage. *They're getting away, but at least I'll have that scar-faced bastard.* The Dakota was out of range in a matter of seconds. Angrily he ordered his men to quit wasting ammunition. Sending back for his Land-Rover, he heard the sound of another engine. For a second he thought it was the plane, then he saw a jeep taking off and heading south.

Casey had gone through the other end of the hangar and had found the mechanic's jeep. Tumbling into it, he hit the starter and was relieved when the engine turned over. If Mtuba wanted him, he'd have to go a bit farther.

Gaining altitude, Harrison made another pass over the field, reluctant to leave. He saw the plume of dust thrown up by the jeep as it sped south down the road, then took off cross country. Harrison let loose a yell that sent Van racing up to the cockpit, thinking they'd been hit. Pointing out the tiny speck of the jeep below, with its tail of dust, both men laughed and cried at once, bellowing out the smashed window, "Go! Go! Go!"

Van slapped Harrison on the back. "I knew they couldn't get him! That big-nosed son of a bitch will live forever, I tell you. He'll live forever."

Mtuba had no future. If he returned to Kimshaka, his fate was certain, and there was no place on the continent where he would be welcome now that the mercenaries had gotten away with his Chinese.

A cloud of reddish dust rose over a field behind a small hill. There went the source of his troubles, still heading south. Then that was the way he would go too. This game had to be played out to its conclusion, and if he was to die, then he would at least have had the satisfaction of winning part of the game. His trucks would be useless in following the jeep. He took with him a sergeant named Tobutam, with whom he had worked before, and two of his best trained men. They took off in the Land-Rover. He told the rest of his force to head back across the border to Kimshaka after concealing the bodies of their dead. The dead mercenaries would be left where they fell. Let the local authorities try to figure out what had happened. He had no further use for the rest of his men, they had failed him miserably. It was fortunate that none of them knew what his fate would be if he returned with them. To them, and to the men he was taking with him, he was still in command and would be obeyed.

Topping his tanks from the supplies at the hangar, Mtuba made one last decision before leaving the Dutch strip. He had the three Africans in the tool cage shot. It would be best if there were no one left alive to tell what happened and who was involved. It might buy him a few more hours before word went out that he was to be killed. If nothing else, Mtuba was a realist, and he was a fighter who would not quit until he was totally beaten.

Taking the wheel of the Land-Rover himself, he left the strip behind, following the tracks of the jeep in the dust. If the mercenary kept heading the way he was going, and if he stayed off the few roads, it was unlikely they would run into anyone other than a few farmers.

The mercenary could, of course, head east and try to cross over to Rhodesia at Lake Victoria. But if he went that way, he would probably run into armed patrols who would be asking questions about the slaughter at the airstrip.

If Casey had extra cans of gas with him, and drove all night, and could find a way across the Zambezi River, he could be at the fringes of the Okovanggo swamps by the next morning after crossing the Caprivi Strip into Botswana. If he made it that far, then he'd be able to pick up the road connecting Maun to Francistown on the Rhodesian border, or he could go cross country from Nata to Bulawayo in Rhodesia. There, the border was not heavily guarded, with hundreds of miles of mostly unsettled open land and very few men to patrol them.

It didn't matter to Mtuba which choice Casey opted for. He would meet him at the end of their trail. He knew this land well, certainly much better than did the white hireling. There were shortcuts he could take to intercept his prey.

Casey pushed down the jeep's windshield and ignored the pain in his leg. The wound had already started to close up. He'd stopped just long enough to put a battle dressing on it, then moved on. The pain would pass; right now he had to get some distance between himself and the N.F.L.K.

Weighing more heavily on his mind than his own escape were his men. He worried about them. Were they going to make it? And if he were taken, how long would it be before he would see Yu Li again? Nearly running over a warthog burrow, he pushed those thoughts aside. He couldn't afford to split his concentration.

The dry wind whipping at his face felt good as he hit a long flat stretch of open ground that permitted him the luxury of deliberate thought again.

Now, perhaps, some breaks would come his way. By now Mtuba and his soldiers were probably across the border, back in Kimshaka. There would be no reason for them to continue the chase now that Major Xaun was out of their reach. Casey was worried about Beidemann's wounds, but their medic was a good man, and now that Harrison had his plane, they should be safe in Rhodesia in just a couple of hours. There Beidemann could get to a hospital, and Major Xaun could be turned over to the proper officials. Casey knew that all he had to do was avoid getting captured by the local authorities. They would undoubtedly ask some very difficult questions about what had happened at the airstrip, questions that he would prefer not to answer from the confines of some stinking cell where he would probably end up having to spend many years. He had come to the same conclusions about his own course of action as had Mtuba. He would have to avoid any towns on his route, at least until he was across the Zambezi.

He drove for three hours until, from a hill overlooking a valley, he saw a city. Checking his map, he knew it had to be Mankoya. He was making good time. Getting out of the jeep to refuel, he was glad that the Dutch mechanic had kept his vehicle fully serviced and ready for the field, as did many in these lands where gas stations were often a hundred or more miles apart. Lifting one of the jerry cans of gas from its rack, he looked back the way he had come.

"Aw, shit!" he said, nearly dropping the precious can. From the hill he stood on, he could see a glint of light about three and a half miles to the north. The afternoon sun was reflecting off the glass of a vehicle. He didn't have to see the men in it to know who was following him. Mtuba! He didn't understand why the man was still after him. It didn't make any sense. *Maybe the bastard just went nuts,* he thought. Whatever the reason, Casey couldn't take the time to figure it out until after he crossed the Zambezi. For now, he'd just have to run.

Resigned to what had to be, he filled his tanks and put the empty cans back into their racks; he might have a need for them later. Taking a candy bar out of the pack thrown him from the plane, he ate it slowly, letting the chocolate dissolve in his mouth. He chased it down with a single swallow of tepid, tasteless water. He was tired, and there was no one to help him with the driving. As it was, he had not been fully asleep since the night before they'd boarded the planes for the jump into Dzhombe's palace. How long had that been? It was getting hard to keep track of time. Three days or four? Climbing back into the seat, he turned the flat nose of the old four-cylinder jeep to the east, where he'd avoid Mankoya and cross the road leading from it to Lusaka. From there he'd turn south again.

Mtuba turned the wheel of the Land-Rover over to his sergeant. He would need his rest. He had seen the jeep and knew that he was right in his earlier judgments. After he passed the Lusaka road, he'd have his man swing wide to the east and take another road not on the map that would cut around until he was able to get in front of the mercenary. After Mankoya, there was only one way the foreigner could go to cross the river between Sesheke and Livingstone, and he, Mtuba, would be waiting for him at the Zambezi crossing.

Montfort called van Janich at home, trying to control the excitement in his voice. "Sir, I have good news. Our friends in Rhodesia have just notified me that they have received a radio message from Romain's pilot, the crazy Englishman, Harrison. They say they have wounded on board and have brought me a special guest to speak to. Maybe this is our lucky day, and we'll get some straight answers for a change."

He listened to van Janich's excited response on the other end of the line, nodded his head, and continued. "I have asked our friends to send those of Mr. Romain's unit who are not seriously wounded on to us. They should be arriving by jet in less than two hours."

CHAPTER EIGHTEEN

Montfort and van Janich were not at all pleased with what Van and Harrison told them, nor were they satisfied with the answers given by Major Xaun, who now claimed to have no knowledge at all of any plans for North Korean volunteers to be given to the N.F.L.K. to offset the Cuban presence in Angola. Now that Xaun was in what he felt were more civilized hands, he put on a passive expression and calmly denied everything, saying only that he had been sent to the N.F.L.K. as no more than an observer and just happened to be with the unit that met Casey's men outside of Kimshaka City. In fact, he claimed it was the mercenaries who'd started the firefight, though for

what reasons he couldn't say. He suggested they might
be in the pay of the Russians.

Harrison and Van didn't give a damn what the Chinese
said or what van Janich did with him. They wanted to
know what was going to be done for Casey. It had been
three hours since they'd been brought from a landing
field outside of Zawi, northwest of Salisbury.

They'd set down on the first strip that was near a town
that looked large enough to have a hospital. That was
where Beidemann and the other wounded mercs were
now. They were under close guard by members of the
Selous Scouts in order to make certain that their presence
was kept secret from the outside world. When they were
able to be moved, they would be returned to Malaya by
a plane with diplomatic status. All the others were already
on their way out of Africa after their debriefing by van
Janich. Only Van and Harrison stayed behind. They'd
refused to go until they knew about Casey and Beidemann, who was still under the surgeon's knife in the
community hospital at Zawi.

Van Janich didn't push the issue. It was possible the
mercs might still have some information to give him.
Van Janich had to believe Harrison and Van; there were
too many things going on in Kimshaka that made their
statements make sense. It was now clear why relations
with the N.F.L.K. had suddenly turned from their normal
chilly state to one of near freezing. As far as Major Xaun
was concerned, van Janich knew how to handle him. The
Front said they knew nothing of any Chinese in their
country. Therefore, Major Xaun did not officially exist.
Once Xaun realized that he had no protection of any
kind, he'd either talk or truly disappear forever from the
face of the earth.

Harrison returned van Janich's attention to his and Van's concern. "What about Casey? Are you just going to write him off after he's done your dirty work for you?"

"We are going to do no such thing," Montfort answered with quiet sincerity. "We always live up to our end of a bargain. And we do believe what you've told us about the N.F.L.K. and the Chinese is true." Moving over to a large wall map of Africa, he asked Harrison to come and point out where they were when they took the Dutch plane. That was another problem to be taken care of, but money could buy many kinds of cooperation, and this particular mining company had been negotiating with them for some mineral rights. Now it looked as if they might have a very good chance of getting them.

Harrison pointed out where the field was located. It was just outside Kasempa. "Here. When we last saw him, he was in a jeep heading south."

Montfort looked at van Janich, who nodded, making an unspoken agreement.

"Mr. Harrison, we cannot go into another country with armed men to search for your leader. The situation is too politically explosive right now. Besides which, there is a lot of country out there and a dozen ways he could go. What we can do, however, is have everyone on duty at the Rhodesian border be on the alert for him. If he crosses into Rhodesia, they'll get him back to us as they did you and your comrades. If he goes south to Botswana and tries to cross the Zambezi, we'll have native agents on the lookout. Sooner or later he'll have to come to one place or another where we'll be able to help him. The moment we have a fix on him, we'll have a pickup arranged either by land or air. If he can just keep out of official hands until then, we'll be able to help. If he is arrested and jailed in Barotseland, then we'll have to pull a lot of strings. The most important leverage we have is the information you've given us about the Chinese and the North Koreans. While some of our black African neighbors hate us, we all have one thing in common: none of us wants any more foreigners in our countries trying to take over." Montfort knew the feelings Van and Harrison had for their leader. In the short time he had known Casey Romain, he had recognized qualities in him that drew one to the man. Whether one agreed with him or not, one had the feeling that he was basically a good man, although a bit strange.

Trying to reassure them was not easy. "Look here, chaps, there's nothing more you can do for now. Go and get some rest. As soon as we get any word at all, I promise I'll send for you. We are not going to leave your man in the lurch."

Van and Harrison knew Montfort was right. They were very tired, and there might come a time soon when they'd need to have clear heads and eyes. They would sleep, then they'd be back.

The night was clear, the stars brilliant. Warm winds came from the south off the Kalahari. There was no humidity, just a dry movement of air that had no taste in it of the rains yet to come. Between Casey and the Kalahari were two bodies of water, both of them now low: the Zambezi River and the Okovanggo swamps. Casey didn't want to go as far as the swamps and didn't think he had enough fuel to make it there anyway. More than likely, if he got as far as the Zambezi, he'd have to strike out on foot until he found another mode of transportation. The jeep had started to give him some trouble. It was running hot and missing. If it stalled out at the wrong time, it could mean big trouble if Mtuba or the local authorities got too close to him. Thinking of Mtuba, he realized he hadn't seen him since he'd refueled near Mankoya. But somehow he didn't think he'd lost him. He had a very strong premonition that he and Mtuba would meet again, and it would be very soon. He just hoped it wouldn't be beyond the Okovanggo, in the desert where the bones of thousands lay and where only the Bushmen were truly at home.

From Mulobezi, a two-hour drive could take him either to Livingstone and the crossing over the Victoria Falls into Rhodesia or over the Mulobezi Bridge where he could go on to Sesheke and ferry it over the Zambezi. Neither option was particularly appealing to Casey, for he was growing increasingly weary. His eyes felt as though tiny, gritty, red-hot coals were nestling under the lids. He would have to sleep soon, and that would be dangerous. But if he didn't, he'd probably end up wrecking the jeep. Sleeping wasn't something he wanted to do on this side of the border, but he had to. Pulling the jeep over to the side of the trail he'd been following, he tried to cover it with brush to keep it from being seen by casual eyes. If Mtuba or someone were really looking for him, there was no way he could conceal the miles of tracks the jeep's tires had laid behind him. It was just a chance he'd have to take.

When he had the jeep covered, he took his pack and weapons and moved a couple of hundred yards away from it to the south, where he'd be able to run for it if the jeep were found. This way he'd still be heading in the right direction.

Smoke drifted over the trees, and Casey could smell

meat cooking. His mouth watered at the windborne menu.
The savory smell came from a village that was one of
the Tonga kraals. Cattle, distantly related to the Brah-
man, were being roasted for some celebration or other.

Climbing up into the branches of a tree, he made a
nest where he could at last close his eyes. Twisting his
body to fit the angle of the tree and its branches, he
placed his G-3 over his chest with the strap around his
neck, then slung the pack high on his left arm. He was
taking no chances on dropping anything if he moved
while asleep. Looking at the night sky through the
branches, he tried to set his mental clock for no more
than three or four hours of sleep, one for each day he'd
been awake. When he awoke it would still be dark, and
he'd be able to make the Zambezi crossing between Livingstone and Sesheke by dawn. He was still thinking
about the Zambezi when he blinked and was out.

Mtuba pushed the Land-Rover hard. It had a larger
motor and more power than the smaller and older American jeep. After he'd left Mankoya, he cut over and drove
alongside the Kafue River until he came to the asphalt
road between Lusaka and Livingstone. Being an African,
he attracted little attention even in his uniform, which
was not an uncommon sight to the villagers and travelers
on the road.

Six miles north of Livingstone he left the paved road
and turned due west, which was how he believed Casey
had gone. It was the only decent track a wheeled vehicle
could traverse going south from Mulobezi. If he was
right, and they'd picked up the extra time by using the
paved road, then he would be well in front of his prey.
Now he just had to wait for the pale, fish-bellied hired
killer to appear.

They reached the Zambezi crossing two hours before dawn. At that time of year—during the dry season—the water level of that section was so low that the river could be crossed on foot. Anywhere else on the river, however, one would still require a bridge or ferry to get to the Botswana side. *This has to be the place*, he thought. Sending his sergeant and two men out to check the ground around the riverbank, Mtuba leaned back in the seat and closed his eyes.

He awoke at the sound of booted feet on dry leaves. The sergeant reported, "Sir, we went up and down the river for three kilometers in each direction. There is no sign that the jeep or any other vehicle has crossed. The riverbed shows only the tracks of bare feet. The one you want has not come this way."

Mtuba stretched his arms out expansively. "Not come this way *yet*, you mean. But he will, he will. Now get the Land-Rover out of sight and place yourselves along the track so that I can have some warning if he comes while I'm sleeping. I wouldn't wish to be late for our meeting. It has been too long delayed."

Saluting, the sergeant left to carry out his orders. He sent two men down the track with flashlights. One was to go half a mile, and the other was to go a mile; each would use his flashlight to signal the approach of the mercenary. This way, they would be in front of and behind him when he came to the river. The sergeant didn't understand what was so important about this one man, but if Mtuba wanted him, then that was the way it would have to be. Mtuba had a reputation for getting exactly what he wanted, no matter at whose expense.

Casey nearly rolled out of his tree. The cough of a hunting leopard sounded as if it were right in his ear.

The cry came once more, then the frogs took over with
their interminable whistling, clucking, and croaking. Africa had hundreds of different species of tree-dwelling
frogs and toads, and Casey thought that most of them
had to be no more than twenty feet away. He peered up
at the sky, then checked his watch. It was 0400 hours;
the leopard had awakened him right on time. Grunting
from a cramp in his leg, he shinnied down the trunk of
the tree to the ground. He listened and looked, then
unzipped his trousers to ease the pressure on his bladder.
After he finished, he gave a satisfied sigh and rubbed
his eyes, glad the worst of the soreness in them was
gone. He made his way back to where his jeep waited
for him. He watched it for a few minutes, then circled
around behind it to make certain no one was waiting in
ambush for him. All clear. Removing the brush, he hit
the starter once, twice, three times, working the gas pedal
up and down each time before he could get it to start.
The motor sounded rougher than ever. Jolting it into gear,
he got it back out onto the track. Just a few more hours
and he'd be at the crossing. Once on the other side, he
didn't think he'd have any trouble getting to one of the
Rhodesian border posts. It was hard not to think about
the others, especially Beidemann, but he had to keep his
concentration on the thin trail.

As he neared the river, the foliage grew thicker. Overhead the trees came together, often forming a living tun-
nel that blocked out the starlight from the night sky; even
if there'd been a full moon, he doubted its glow could
have penetrated the leaves. The rattling of his motor was
accompanied by the increasing chatter of animals in the
branches. Several times he heard howls that made the
hackles rise on the back of his neck. At an occasional

break in the trees, he could sometimes see hundreds of small shapes leaping from branch to branch. Monkeys, frightened of something hunting them, chattered angrily at him from high above.

Four miles from the Zambezi crossing, the motor of the jeep coughed and died. Cursing, Casey raised the hood and tried to adjust the carburetor, then tried to clear out the fuel line. Nothing worked. He tried to start it until the battery finally gave up the ghost. There was nothing to do now but hoof it. At least he didn't have much further to go. Pushing the jeep off the trail into a clump of brush, he shouldered his rifle and pack, and got a move on. He tried to maintain the distance-eating stride of the professional soldier, but the potholes and vines crossing the road kept tripping him, so he gave it up. He just moved along at an easy gait, still having to favor his leg a bit. The wound had closed, but it did give him a twinge now and then.

The rebel soldier at the one-mile mark from the river was listening for a vehicle. He knew he'd hear it before he saw it. That was what killed him. He got careless and lit a cigarette. That small red glow caught the eye of the one he'd been waiting for.

Casey had been deep in thought. The night was a heavy cover that paced each step. He wasn't afraid of it. He had been in darkness too many times before. It was more like a companion that had shared many troubles. He thought he could smell the water of the Zambezi coming toward him on a light breeze that rustled the leaves overhead and evaporated the sweat on his face. Periodically he would stop and listen, turning in all directions, then he'd continue on his way once more. It

was during one of these stops that he saw a reddish glow
wink at him, fade, then wink again and disappear. He
knew immediately what it was; someone in the brush in
front of him was smoking. Casey knew he wasn't through
with Mtuba yet. Moving to the sides of the track, his
camouflage uniform blended in with the thin light breaking through gaps in the leafy canopy overhead. Taking
his time, he silently worked his way toward where he
had seen the glow. Patience was needed. Very carefully,
each foot was placed one in front of the other as he
searched the ground for any dried twigs or leaves that
could give him away to whoever was waiting. He kept
to the shadows or to the cover of trees and brush where
his camouflage uniform granted him a degree of invisi-
bility in the early dawn. He crept closer until he could
smell the scent of burning tobacco.

The ash glowed once more. Turning his head slightly
to the side, Casey looked out from the corner of his eye,
using his peripheral vision to pinpoint his target. There
he was! A man was leaning casually against the bole of
a vine-wrapped tree, his weapon resting against his leg,
one hand cupping the cigarette. Casey unslung the rifle
from his shoulder, then took his bayonet from its sheath
and moved in closer. Breathing shallowly through his
mouth so he wouldn't tip off the careless watcher, he
came to within arm's length of the tree. He waited a
moment, then looked and listened to see if there was
anyone else around. Satisfied no one else was there, he
grabbed the soldier and covered his mouth with his left
hand as the bayonet slid across the man's throat. He
pulled the soldier to him, holding him to his chest as he
applied pressure to the blade. He forced the finely honed
edge in so deeply it nearly severed the man's head, slicing

through the carotid artery and jugular vein. The blood drained from the soldier's head so quickly that consciousness left him immediately, and death followed only a heartbeat later.

Casey let the body down easy. He wiped the blood from his hand on the man's tunic, then rolled him over to get a look at the face. From the uniform he knew he was right; this was one of Mtuba's men. The man's cigarette glowed and winked in the grass, and Casey ground it out under his heel. Then he dragged the body further back into the trees and placed it under some bushes.

He went back to the road and tried to figure out what Mtuba's plan was. If this man was placed on the trail, then there were probably others. But how many? He was sure that all Mtuba had with him were the men he could carry in the Land-Rover. That meant no more than three or four besides Mtuba. Three or four, less one. He guessed the flashlight the soldier had with him was probably used for signaling.

Casey went back to the body and took the flashlight. There might be a need for it later. Right now he needed to get down the track and avoid anyone waiting for him. It was going to take a bit longer, but he decided he had to stay off the track completely and work his way along the sides through the thick undergrowth and brush.

Checking the sky and his watch, he figured he had one more hour of semidarkness left, but he wasn't certain how much further he'd have to go before reaching the river. It took nearly half an hour for him to cover the next half mile. Once more he had the advantage of a warning, not from a cigarette this time, but from a cough. It was the rasping hack of someone with pneumonia or maybe a touch of TB. A throat tried to clear itself, then

the man spat out a hunk of phlegm. Casey moved toward
him and was nearly on him when the soldier heard the
movement and spun around, his AK-47 at the ready.

"Jambo," Casey whispered to the man, then turned
on his flashlight. The combination of the familiar greet-
ing and the light from the flashlight that his comrade was
supposed to have slowed up the soldier's reactions. By
the time he'd figured it out, it was too late. Casey's
bayonet had taken another victim. He got him with a
straight thrust into the esophagus. Casey's free hand
twisted the man's rifle loose from fingers that were already going to his throat to try and remove the cold steel
thing that had stopped his breath. Casey helped him along
in his efforts. With the man's own rifle, he struck him
on the side of the head, then quickly leaned over the
unconscious body and finished the job. Withdrawing the
knife from the man's throat, he moved it to where he
could strike deep down into the hollow of the neck where
the long blade of the bayonet could reach the upper part
of the man's heart without the danger of being stuck in
a rib or bouncing off bone. Wiping the blade clean, he
resheathed it wishing he knew how many more men were
nearby. There couldn't be more than one or two. From
where he stood he could hear the lapping water. The
Zambezi was just ahead, and he'd give odds that so was
Colonel Mtuba. . . .

CHAPTER NINETEEN

Van Janich was not pleased with the turn of events. Too many things had gone wrong with what should have been a straightforward operation. Dzhombe was dead; but now they had a greater monster to contend with if the Communist Chinese were coming in. Africa was beginning to get very crowded. All that Harrison and the Vietnamese had said was true. Major Xaun had confirmed that, and more. He had not done so willingly, but Sodium Pentothal had taken care of that. Now it was up to the diplomats. Copies of Xaun's statements were already on their way to the capitals of the West and to the member nations of the Federation of African Unity, to which Kimshaka did not belong. But the Federation was certain to be very concerned about the presence of the Chinese and could be effective with the United Nations Security Council. He was sure measures would be taken to prevent any North Koreans from being sent to Kimshaka.

Major Xaun had become more cooperative since his injections, knowing that he could never return home now that he had blown the cover of a very secret and a very expensive operation. He was scheduled for a video taping the following morning. He would reveal on camera the extent of the Chinese plot. It would be quite difficult for the Communists to get anyone to believe their denials of foreign interference once the world saw the video tape.

Even now, van Janich's agents were in Kimshaka gathering hard intelligence about the Chinese presence. Earlier that day van Janich had authorized a raid into Kimshaka to where he knew the N.F.L.K. had a major munitions and arms depot. If he was correct, his men would return with enough weapons and equipment to prove conclusively the degree of Chinese involvement. The United Nations would have to act.

As for the problem of the whereabouts of Casey Romain, van Janich didn't give the man much of a chance. But he would do as he'd promised. He owed him that much. The mercenaries had paid a high price in blood, and now he had the unpleasant task of going over to where Harrison and Van were staying in a safe house and informing them that their friend Gustaf Beidemann had died in the recovery room. It was not something he relished doing, but he felt it deserved to be handled in person. He hoped that he would not have to tell them something similar about their leader.

• • •

Casey lay on his belly. The early morning sun was already causing a mist to rise from the brown waters of the Zambezi. The dampness felt good to his dry mouth and lips. It had been a long night.

Someone had called out a name a few minutes earlier, probably the name of the second man he'd killed. Casey had hoped he would be able to sneak by Mtuba and cross over before the colonel found his men dead, but that chance was now too remote. When Mtuba's man didn't respond to his name being called, Casey distinctly heard the metallic clack of gun bolts being worked.

The flowing water of the river called him. Through the leaves of the bush he was lying behind, he could make out the opposite bank where Botswana lay waiting for him if he could just get across.

Mtuba had moved to where he had cover behind the stump of a giant tree. Fifty yards north, his sergeant was in a similar position behind a clump of smooth boulders. Mtuba was beginning to feel uneasy. Nothing had gone right for him. He knew the merc was close to him, and all he had left was one stupid sergeant. The others had to be dead, or they would have answered the sergeant's hail. He hated the scar-faced man out there as he had never hated anyone or anything in his life. His world was ending because of him. All that he had worked for was but bitter ashes in his mouth. If he was going to die, he would take this one with him before he did. The mist cooled him as it did the man in the brush, but beads of moisture collected on his upper lip.

Now, he thought. *Come to me now! Let us put an end to this thing we have. It has to be done; there is no other way for it to end. Come to me. I am tired of chasing you.* Snapping his fingers to get Sergeant Tobutam's attention, he pointed to the edge of the clearing. He was certain that was where the mercenary would have to come from. He would, if he were in the man's position. He knew his man was out there and hoped he understood what it was that had grown between them in the last few days. He would not be disappointed.

Casey's eyes clicked to the right, away from the road running alongside the river.

Don't be impatient. Casey's thoughts were directed at his unseen adversary. *We've come this far. It won't take much longer. You're a stubborn bastard, Mtuba, I give you that. Why have you come so far to get me? Is it because you let us take the Chinese away from you and you can't go home without him? If so, that puts a different light on things. You're here to make one final gesture. Even if you won, it wouldn't change things for you. You're a dead man....All right, let's see where you are!*

Falling back a step to give himself some more cover, he flicked the selector switch to full auto. He raised the weapon to his shoulder and fired. The rifle bucked against his shoulder like a living thing as he sprayed the edge of the riverbank from left to right. He hit the ground on his side and rolled behind a tree trunk to his left to get away from where he had fired.

Sergeant Tobutam's edgy nerves took over. His finger had been on the trigger of his AK-47 for over thirty minutes, and the sour odor of his own fear wouldn't leave his nostrils. When Casey fired, it was a relief. At last there was something to which he could react! Only one of Casey's rounds hit the boulder Tobutam was behind, but it was enough to set the sergeant off. His finger pulled the trigger, and he returned fire at the place where cordite and flashes of light 'had appeared. Leaves and branches crashed down as Tobutam's bullets cut through trees and brush.

Mtuba held his fire. He was furious at Tobutam. *The stupid ass has given away his position!* And now he'd have to pay for it. He had no doubt the mercenary would kill his man, but maybe that would work to his purpose. Tobutam could now be used as bait. Rolling back down to the edge of the water, Mtuba lowered his body into the river. There were enough boulders, trees, and logs to give him plenty of cover. He moved to where he could whisper and only Tobutam could hear him.

"Good work, Sergeant," he lied. "I think you may have wounded him. I'm sure I heard a grunt of pain after you fired. Just stay where you are. I'm going upstream a bit and will come in behind him. Just keep firing when you see or hear anything. Try to keep his attention to the front. This way we'll have him between us. We'll kill him, and then we can go home."

That sounded good to Tobutam. Especially the going home part. Mtuba did not move as far upstream as Tobutam thought he would, nor did he leave the clump of water-soaked logs he was lying behind to try and get behind the mercenary....

Mtuba waited for the mercenary to kill the sergeant. If he waited long enough, the man would have to come down to the water and check things out. Then he would have him.

Casey kept low as leaves and twigs showered down on him. He saw only one flash of gunfire from a group of boulders to his right. That was all. Was it Mtuba, or

was there more than one man out there? He had the
feeling that Mtuba was too experienced to fall for an old
trick like the one Casey had just pulled. But it was also
possible that he was nervous and tired. Lack of sleep
does strange things to a man's mind and reactions. At
least things were starting to happen. Now he had to keep
the pressure on. He had to get across the river, and as
soon as possible. There was always the chance that their
rifle fire would be heard by someone else. And this
section of the river, while not a major crossing point,
was sure to be patrolled periodically now that the water
level was down. He didn't think the Africans on this side
of the river would have much sympathy for him. They'd
probably side with Mtuba.

Reloading his rifle, Casey snaked his body along,
keeping as low as he could. Most game was spotted by
movement. He would take it easy. He crawled back to
the edge of the trees where a strip of reddish clay ran to
the bank of the river. There was a small clearing that he
would have to cross. Gauging the distance from the edge
of the trees to the boulders, he guessed it to be about
forty yards. Not far, but if a man was good with his
weapon, a guy could get his ass filled with slugs before
he ever reached the shooter. Casey had to figure out how
to get the man behind the boulder into the open where
he could get a shot at him.

There were several tree stumps along the side of the
riverbank that he'd be able to reach if he could just make
the man behind the boulders keep his head down for a
few seconds. Waiting, Casey moved his gaze slowly,
carefully taking in everything he saw, noting anyplace
that could be used for cover by his enemy.

Taking off his pack, he rummaged in it until he found

what he was looking for. Putting the pack back on, he looked long at the boulders before pulling the pin on the grenade. Scooting over to where he'd have enough clearance for a full arm swing, he took a deep breath and extended his right arm back. Turning his body like a corkscrew, his right arm rising over his head, he hurled it with the full force of his back muscles and weight. He knew he wouldn't be able to throw the steel egg far enough to hit the boulders, but that wasn't his plan. While the grenade was still in the air, he rose to his feet, moved out of the trees toward the riverbank, and opened fire, spraying the boulders with bullets. Sergeant Tobutam winced as granite splinters peppered his face. It being his turn to fire, Tobutam stuck his head out from behind his boulder, rifle to his shoulder, eye to the sight, as the grenade landed twenty feet in front of him.

Casey hit the ground, rolling behind a half-rotted tree trunk as the grenade went off. Before the noise of the explosion faded into silence completely, he was back up and over the trunk, moving toward the boulders.

Sergeant Tobutam nearly lost an eye when the grenade went off. The blast had startled him so badly that he'd rammed the sight of his rifle into his eye when he jerked back for cover behind his granite shelter.

Mtuba lowered himself further into the water when Casey fired, raising his head only after the grenade went off. Moving his rifle to where he could try a shot, he saw Casey going after Tobutam.

Tobutam knew he was outclassed. The mercenary was going to kill him if he didn't do something. He did the only logical thing he could do under the circumstances. He threw down his AK-47 and raised his hands above his head as he stood away from the boulder.

Mtuba swore at the ignorant, stupid beast. *The god-damned fool's in my line of fire!* He couldn't get a shot at Casey with the sergeant standing in the way. He too did the only logical thing he could do under the circumstances. He put five rounds into Tobutam's back, blasting out the man's chest where the rounds exited. One of the copper-nosed slugs that passed through Sergeant Tobutam's body hit the stock of Casey's G-3, knocking it from his hands.

Casey's right hand was numbed from the impact of the bullet. Instinctively hitting the deck, he rolled behind the boulders that Tobutam now had no use for. Reaching around the boulder, he dragged back Tobutam's automatic and nearly lost a hand in the attempt. Mtuba put the rest of his magazine into a long, hosing burst, hit the magazine release, and reloaded.

Casey checked his new weapon. A full clip! He would have liked to have taken the extra magazines for the AK-47 off Tobutam's body, but that would have exposed him too much. What should he do? Only a few seconds away was the other side of the river and Botswana. *Well, if it worked once, maybe it'll work again,* he thought. Shrugging off his pack, he removed his last two grenades.

Hanging the Kalashnikov assault rifle around his neck, he checked the rounds in his pistol, jacked a round in the chamber, and put it back in its holster. Pulling the pins on the grenades, he held one in each hand. His back against the boulder, he leaned out just far enough to look upriver. Mtuba fired a single shot that whizzed past his head. Casey leaned back out of sight and sucked air into his lungs. He had to time this just right. Turning to kneel, his head against the boulder, he heaved the first grenade over the top and slowly counted to five. Exploding in the water fifteen feet away from Mtuba, the majority of the grenade's force was absorbed by the river. But it was enough to cause Mtuba to submerge his head in the water, his ears ringing.

Casey was out and running, the other grenade flying free from his hand. Mtuba rose up, shaking his head to free his eyes of water. He saw Casey moving toward the river. Before he could get his weapon ready to fire at the target, he saw another small, round object hurtling through the air at him. Frantically he sank down behind his logs, covering his face and eyes with a forearm. This time the explosion was much closer. Blood ran from his nose, his upper lip ripped to the cheekbone by a steel splinter. But another seven or eight seconds had passed. A man could cover a lot of ground in that amount of time. Casey was nearly to the Botswana side of the river. Standing, Mtuba shook himself like a dog and fired from the hip, his soaked AK-47 smoking with steam. Mtuba cried out in rage as his bullets walked through the river toward the back of his target. Then nothing! The magazine was empty! Panicking at the thought of losing his quarry, he reloaded with angry, awkward fingers that wouldn't do what he wished.

Casey rolled behind a fallen tree trunk on the Botswana side of the river, whipping back around to face the way he had come. Peeking over the top of the log, he hoped he would see that Mtuba had turned around and quit the chase. It was senseless for him to continue it. The game was over, and all the players should go home. No such luck. The maniac was still coming.

Casey sighted him with the AK-47. There was no way he could miss. Mtuba worked a round into the chamber from a fresh magazine and started wading across the river. Blood dripped from his nose, mouth, and ears. Casey knew the man was on the ragged edge of madness.

Wildly, Mtuba fired a ten-round burst from the hip, missing his target by yards.

"Go back! It's over! There's no need for any more killing!" Casey called out to him.

"It's not done with! Not yet!" Mtuba screamed and fired again. This time the rounds hit much closer.

Casey knew he had little choice in the matter. Lowering his aim to Mtuba's belly, he started to take in the slack on the trigger.

Casey's sheltering tree trunk nearly exploded as heavy machine gun bullets tried to tear it apart. From across the river, a motorized patrol with a fifty-caliber mounted on their jeep blasted away at him.

"Aw, shit!" Casey scrambled backward, dropping over a small rise where his body was hidden from the gunner. Crawling quickly to put some more distance between himself and the long reach of the heavy machine gun, he knew he should have blown Mtuba away. Now he'd still have that crazy son of a bitch on his ass.

The patrol had come upon the scene prepared to fight. They'd heard the grenade explosions from a mile away. When they saw Mtuba going after the white man in camouflage, they picked their side in a hurry. They had heard reports of white mercenaries in the area and were eager to add one to their tally. It would mean instant promotion to bring one in—dead or alive.

CHAPTER TWENTY

Montfort met Van and Harrison near the military airfield. It was a clear, warm day with just enough heat to cast a thin sheen of moisture on foreheads and upper lips.

Montfort whisked away a bothersome fly with a wave of his hand. "I have some news for you."

Harrison and Van stopped. A C-119 taxied down the runway to their left. Harrison spoke for both of them. "Casey? Have you found him?"

Montfort shook his head. "No. We haven't found him, but we have just had a report come in that early this morning there was a firefight of some kind near the Zambezi crossing. From what we've been told, there

were several casualties, all dead, and all wearing the
uniform and insignia of the N.F.L.K. We are waiting
for more information now. It should be coming in within
the next hour. I brought you out here to be near the
airfield. I presume that if we spot him, you'll want to
be in on the pickup."

Van began to get excited, and wanted them to get a
plane and go up immediately. Montfort tried to calm him
down a little.

"We can't just take off and fly around in circles. It
would be senseless. We have to wait. I don't even know
for certain that he was responsible for the casualties on
the Zambezi."

Harrison scratched a sore place under his armpit. "I
don't think there's much doubt about that. Too many
pieces fit, and you don't know Casey like we do. But
you're right about just flying around. So, if you don't
mind, we have a funeral to attend. Then we'll come back
and wait at the tower until you find out more."

Montfort shifted his feet, feeling a bit uneasy and
guilty. "Yes, I know. My driver will take you in the
Bentley. I would go with you, but I think I should stay
here, just in case."

Harrison and Van nodded their understanding, and
left. They said nothing on the way to Victoria Military
Cemetery, and the driver left them to their thoughts. Van
Janich had arranged it so Beidemann could be buried
with other fallen soldiers. It was an act of compassion,
considering the dead man had once been on the opposite
side, but somehow, from what van Janich had learned
of Beidemann from Harrison and Van, the big German
had never been an enemy.

They were greeted by van Janich, who had canceled
several appointments to be there.

"Welcome, my friends. We are ready to begin." There was no chaplain at the grave site to say fine things over the dead. The eulogy would be spoken by a man who'd never met him. Perhaps that was the best way.

Van and Harrison stood silently by the grave. Behind them, an honor guard of Border Scouts stood ready with FN rifles to fire the last salute.

Van Janich removed his garrison cap, cleared his throat, and searched for the right words.

"I know that there is another who would say the right things about this man. Since he is not here, I will do the best I can for one I did not know personally but feel I have known. For Gustaf Beidemann was a soldier. In that, we here are all the same. From different countries and cultures, religions and beliefs, yes. But we are all soldiers, and it is fitting that we send this man to whatever afterlife he may or may not have believed in, with the honor we would wish shown to ourselves. For in honoring him, we honor ourselves."

Overhead a flight of pink herons flew to the west to search for nesting and feeding grounds in the Okovanggo swampland.

Van Janich felt a growing lump in his chest as he continued.

"I believe that I would have liked this man if I had had the chance to know him. From his comrades I have learned something of him and know that he was a hard man without being cruel, a fighter who did not kill for pleasure, yet loved the fight. In his homeland, the legends tell of Valhallah, where the heroes who fell in battle would be taken by the Valkyries to the Great Hall of Odin where they would feast and battle throughout eternity. I think that is the heaven we should wish for him. . . . For all of us, I end these proceedings with words from his homeland: *Ich hat eine Kameraden; bessern findst du nicht*—Once I had a comrade; a better one you could not find."

At the command of a lieutenant, the honor guard raised their weapons and fired a volley into the clear sky of Africa, and Gus Beidemann was lowered into his grave.

Van and Harrison held back their tears. They knew Beidemann would not have wanted them to feel sorrow for his death, for he had died the way he had chosen. What greater decision can a man make than to choose the manner of his own death?

Their driver waited to return them to the airfield. Another flight of herons made a half circle and headed after the first.

Casey's mouth was dry and foul-tasting. He'd covered about six miles from the river crossing and wondered where Mtuba was. He didn't think the man had given up on him. For the first hour he'd made every effort to cover his tracks and conceal his movements. Then he had decided that if Mtuba could still trail him after all his evasive actions, then the best thing he could do was to keep moving.

Placing the AK-47 across his back, he settled into an easy, distance-eating jog. He ran across a wide plain where lions hunted in waist-high yellow grass, and let his mind drift away. Separating his body from its actions, it seemed as if he were not the one running; he was only an observer on a high place looking down at the lone figure crossing the yellow plain. He didn't change his stride or pay any attention to the snake he nearly stepped on. It just wasn't there, nor were the lions or the herd of zebra they hunted.

He had no idea how far he'd run when at last he stumbled and fell facedown on the ground. His mouth was pressed against the earth, his breath blowing up small clouds of dust where he breathed against the dry soil.

Slowly he let his body regain control of itself. His breathing slowed; his heart eased its pounding. A flickering shadow flew quickly over his body, momentarily blocking out the burning rays of the sun. A flight of herons ignored the prone, sweat-soaked figure beneath them. They were above the cares of the common world. Up high, they soared where they were the masters.

Staggering back onto his feet, he shaded his eyes and looked ahead of him. Wavering in the distance, riding the heat waves, a forest beckoned him to the coolness of its cover. Coolness that Casey knew was only a mirage. As he turned around to the west, the breeze shifted slightly. A chill rippled over the exposed skin of his face and chest. His jacket stuck to his back. The salt from his pores was already drying to a white powder.

At the Zambezi crossing, the border patrol had wished Mtuba luck in his hunt. And it *was* a hunt. As he ran, he began to strip away his clothes to let his body breath free and clean without coverings, as nature had intended.

Climbing to the top of a termite hill, he looked across the veldt. His naked body felt good stripped of the trappings of Western culture. His nakedness had set him free. It no longer mattered that all he had worked for since he was a young man was gone. He had come full circle. Once he had picked up the spoor of Casey's trail, he let his mind and soul slide back to his beginnings. Only his weapons were of this century. His body was dark and lean, attracting the rays of the sun into his pores as if he fed on them. He had let himself become the primal hunter who would not stop until he had killed. He let his instincts guide him. He smelled the air and earth. Tasting the wind, he knew he was on the right trail.

Several times he had passed others on the plain, herdsmen moving their goats and cattle to water. They avoided his glazed eyes. He in turn asked nothing of them; he knew where to go.

Lifting his gaze to the heavens, his mind was a blank. A flight of herons began to descend to a distant green spot on the horizon where the waters of the Okovanggo marshland offered them refuge. His quarry was not to be found there. Slowly, ever so slowly, he looked across the yellow plain. There! The man was only a tiny speck in the distance, but Mtuba knew it was him.

Leaping from the ten-foot-high termite hill, he ran, light and swift, wishing he had an assegai rather than this unclean weapon made in distant China. It didn't belong here. But he had no choice, and he would use it, although it would not be the same as if he could let good, honest steel drink the blood of he whom he hunted. Then would he cry *"Ngadla!"* saying to the gods, "I have eaten!"

Casey removed his shirt, tying it around his waist. It felt good to let his hot body cool down. Sucking in several deep breaths of air and letting them out slowly, he regained control of his breathing, and the trembling in his legs and stomach eased. Starting off, he tried to figure out how far he could have come and how far it would be to the Rhodesian border. On a map, distance is one thing, but when you have to walk it, it's something altogether different. Overhead, the sun had passed the midday mark and was slowly settling into its afternoon descent. He knew that even with his best time, it would take two, maybe three days to reach the frontier. He was coming to a region of heavy trees and some jungle. He'd have to stop soon after nightfall. In the dark he knew he would lose his way and waste precious time going around in circles.

Checking himself, he changed his pattern of movement to one of walking for two minutes and running for two minutes, an easy pace that didn't drain him of his strength. Just before entering the trees, he came upon the day-old carcass of a grown zebra left to ripen a bit in the sun. The animal had been killed by a half-grown leopard who didn't have the strength to haul the heavy animal's body up into the trees to feed on, as an adult would have done.

Claiming his right to the food, he beat off a pack of vultures and marabou storks who squawked angrily at his intrusion. The birds moved away to wait. They understood the pecking order. Cutting off a large chunk from the rear leg, Casey took his meat and left the scavengers to clean up.

An hour later the tableau was repeated. Mtuba took his share of meat, checked the signs on the earth, and moved out. He was getting close again. That night he would hunt while his prey slept or made camp. There was no doubt in his mind that he would be able to find that which he sought, even in the total darkness of the jungle.

CHAPTER TWENTY-ONE

Van and Harrison stayed at the airfield tower all that day. Planes came and went as the controllers directed them on their approaches and takeoffs. Montfort was with them, and van Janich stopped by twice. The only report to come in was a confirmation that indeed it had been a white man in a camouflage uniform at the crossing. That was more than enough for all of them. The only thing that bothered van Janich was that his agents had said that the border patrol had let a member of the N.F.L.K. go across into Botswana after the mercenary. To Van and Harrison, this was not a great thing to worry about; Casey could take care of himself. If he'd made it that far, then he would go all the way to Rhodesia. As for the man chasing him, if he was even half smart, he'd quit and go back home. Van made the comment to Montfort that whoever was chasing Casey had to be insane. When Montfort asked Van why he thought that, he got a flat, dry, "You have to be crazy to go after Casey."

Montfort thought that the Vietnamese might be right.

An hour after sunset, the major was called to the phone. Van watched him closely, trying to read his face for clues. Replacing the receiver, Montfort turned, and for the first time since Harrison and Van had made it back, he smiled.

"I think we have a fix on him."

Harrison and Van rushed at him, each asking a dozen questions until he finally had to shout, "Shut up a minute and I'll be able to tell you!" When the two had settled down, he filled them in. "I was just informed that Casey was seen today by some tribesmen. He was heading east. I imagine he'll hole up some place tonight, but if he keeps up his pace, he'll be out of the forest and at the Rhodesian border by tomorrow, possibly before nightfall."

Harrison and Van began to whoop it up again but were silenced by Montfort's upraised hand. "There's one more thing. According to the natives, there's an African on his trail with a rifle of some kind."

Van grinned. "Then that's the African's bad luck. Now what do we do?"

Montfort indicated the door. "Why, we go after him of course! Van Janich has arranged for us to take an army helicopter and move near the frontier. We'll refuel at a Rhodesian station and be sitting on the border waiting for him in the morning."

• • •

The floor of the forest was not a good spot. There were too many things that creeped and crawled. Even if they didn't bite, they'd still keep him awake all night.

"Well, I suppose it's time to make like Tarzan again," Casey muttered as he climbed up the nearest tree that had branches strong enough to hold his weight. Once he made his nest of leaves and branches, he dined on raw zebra and wished heartily that he had a cold bottle of beer with which to wash down the rank, tough flesh. He'd eaten worse in his time, however, and that was his only complaint as he tore at the meat with strong teeth.

After eating he pulled his knees up to his chest and placed one arm over a supporting branch to keep from falling out if he turned over in his sleep. Before closing his eyes, he thought about Beidemann, wondering if he'd made it. They had lost too many men on this mission that he liked: Jeremy Fitzhugh, Ali ben Yousef, George. The only good thing that happened was that Van and Harrison had gotten the rest of the men out safely. At least it wasn't a total wipeout. Before sleep took him, his last thoughts were of Yu Li. He felt somehow guilty that she hadn't been in his thoughts more, but the last few days had to be reserved solely for his men. If she knew, she'd understand. It would be good to get back home. . . .

A tree snake slid by his face, flicked out its tongue to taste the aura of the sleeping man, and moved on to seek more familiar prey.

Mtuba moved easily through the brush, just letting his body pick out its own path that would lead him to the

mercenary. His skin prickled with anticipation, an ab-
original awareness. He knew that Casey was near. *Very*
near.

Squatting down on his haunches, he waited. This was
a time for patience. Somewhere near him was that which
he sought. It would make itself known.

His back against a tree, he rocked back and forth on
his heels, trying to make his spirit one with the darkness,
trying to see and feel the forest with his senses. He
listened to the croaking of tree frogs and the cry of night
birds who hunted and mated in the foliage above him.
Beneath his feet, war was being waged endlessly. Huge
horned beetles fought with evil-looking scorpions. Lizards poked into rotten tree stumps to eat the larvae of
wasps. Beneath the rich humus a hundred species of
insect and animal life fought for survival, eating each
other and breeding to perpetuate the cycle of life and
death. Few of nature's creatures died of old age.

Without warning, the night erupted in screeches and
howls. Branches shook and leaves rained down to the
floor of the forest. A hunting cat had killed in the trees
above and was dragging its meal home to feed its cubs.
The hundreds of monkeys who had been quietly feeding
in the trees were protesting its actions.

The sudden howling caused Casey to sit up with a
jerk. His arm slipped off his retaining limb, and his rifle
fell to the earth below.

Mtuba came to his feet. He'd heard clearly the sound
of metal striking wood. Unerringly he moved toward the
place where the sound had originated. In the darkness
his body was no more than another of the thousands of
shadows that flickered for a heartbeat, then were gone.

Swearing between clenched teeth, Casey began to

climb down his tree to retrieve the AK-47. Sliding down the last ten feet, arms and legs holding him close to the trunk, he let out an involuntary grunt when the nub of a broken branch caught him squarely in the crotch.

Mtuba grinned. The sound he had just heard did not come from any beast of the forest. Dropping into a low crouch, he threaded his way between and under broad leaves and through a tangle of vines.

Casey was bending over to pick up the AK-47 when he felt a chill run down his neck and back. It was a feeling that only one who has lived years with death can know. It was a feeling that someone or something was watching, and it wasn't friendly. He had learned long before to trust his instincts in these matters. As he bent over, he kept on going into a roll that took him behind a tree for cover. Suddenly the ear-jarring rattle of automatic rifle fire drove everything else in the forest into silence.

Mtuba ran forward. He knew he'd missed. How the white bastard had known he was behind him didn't matter. He'd still take him.

Casey came up from behind his tree as Mtuba rushed at him. The dark skin of the African made him nearly invisible, but the flashes of fire from the bore of his AK-47 gave him away. Casey tried to cock his own rifle, but the bolt had become jammed when it fell.

In his eagerness to kill, Mtuba lunged forward, believing his target would run from him. Instead, an object flew at him. Teeth broke off at the gums as the butt of the AK-47 came into contact with his mouth. The force of the thrown rifle knocked him flat on his back. Before his mind had fully registered what had happened, his own rifle was jerked from his hands and an incredibly strong set of fingers were around his neck lifting him into the air and slamming his back against the trunk of a tree.

Casey pinned his antagonist there, resisting the urge to simply snap the man's neck. Giving Mtuba a backhand, he knocked him out and let him fall. Using the straps from their rifles, he tied his captive's wrists and ankles. He didn't know why he didn't kill him; maybe he'd seen enough death lately. At least he didn't have to keep looking behind him anymore. Maybe Mtuba might be of interest to Montfort and van Janich. The reason didn't really matter. All he knew was that now he wouldn't get any more sleep.

It was dawn when Casey finally shook Mtuba into awareness; he must have hit him harder than he thought he had. Stiff and tired, he jerked his prisoner to his feet.

"Come on. We have some traveling to do." Mtuba ran a thick tongue over the broken stumps of his teeth and spat out some bloody splinters. He said nothing as Casey broke his jammed rifle against a rock and took Mtuba's good one. Then he untied his legs and used the strap that had been on them for a choke leash around his neck.

"All right, let's go." Casey gave the leash a jerk and led the way. Mtuba suffered his indignities in silence. He would give the white man no satisfaction by pleading.

At noon Casey called a halt by a spring. He let Mtuba rinse out his mouth and drink, then did the same himself. The day was already another scorcher. They'd left the cover of the strip of forest more than an hour before, and were back in open country. He wondered how much further they'd have to go.

Mtuba read his thoughts and spoke for the first time.

"It doesn't matter where we are or what is done to me. You might as well go ahead and kill me. I am ready."

Casey took another mouthful of the tepid water, swirled it through his teeth, and spat it out on the earth. "So you *can* talk after all. Just to make things clear, understand me. I don't really know why I'm taking you alive. Maybe I'm just getting a bit soft, or it might be that you can tell my contractors about your Chinese friends and why they're here."

Mtuba shook his head, his tongue not working properly around his broken teeth. "I will tell them nothing."

Casey picked up his leash and said, "Suit yourself. I really don't give a damn. But tell me one thing: Why did you come after me once the Chinese was out of your reach?"

Mtuba grinned through smashed lips. "You understand nothing! Once the Chinese was gone, it meant I had failed. No matter what the conditions, the responsibility was mine and mine alone. I don't like losing at anything and you have caused me to lose the most important thing in my life: my reason for living. I was to be of service to the new revolution, not just to the cause, but to be a leader of it. That would have brought glory and honor to my name. Now that is gone, and all I had left for a goal in life was you. I really would not have minded being killed if I could have killed you in the process. So, you see, I have been ready to die since we were at the Dutch airstrip. You can do nothing to frighten me or make me cooperate. I am still ready to die!"

Casey gave his leash a jerk to accent his response. "Don't say it too often, or I might help you out."

After marching another hour, a feeling, not quite a sound, vibrated on the hot air. He wasn't sure for a minute, but then there it was. An HU-1b was making straight for them. On its nose Casey could make out the roundels with the national colors of the contractors on it. Waving his rifle, he pulled Mtuba out into a large clearing where they could easily be seen.

The chopper banked and circled the two men. It was making a scan of the area around the clearing to make sure there were no enemy troops in the neighborhood. Seeing none, the pilot changed the chopper's attitude and came straight in, resting its skids on the dusty soil, the spinning rotors creating small whirlwinds. Harrison, Van, and Montfort leapt from the open doors, weapons ready to give cover if needed. Casey pushed Mtuba inside the helicopter, then quickly followed, keeping his hand on the leash. He sat right across from his prisoner. Harrison and Van clambered back on board right behind Montfort, who sat down beside Mtuba. The pilot gave it some more throttle, and the helicopter cleared the ground in an eye-stinging, man-made cyclone of dust, grit, and sand. Casey leaned over, putting his mouth close to Montfort's ear. "I have a present for you if you want him, but he says he'll tell you nothing about the Chinese or anything else."

Montfort gave Mtuba a dirty look that had bullets in it before saying, "That's all right with me. The Chinese you sent us has spilled his guts all over the place. I don't really have any use for this thing." He indicated Mtuba.

Rising up to three thousand feet, the chopper tilted its nose slightly downward and headed north. The beating of the rotors made it difficult to hear. Mtuba sat sullenly between Casey and Van. Yelling above the noise, Casey asked, "How is Gus?" No one said anything. Their expressions were more eloquent than any words could have been. Casey felt his heart drop to his stomach.

Another one gone, the one who had been such a special friend to him.

Mtuba also understood what had taken place, and he began to laugh. Bobbing his head up and down, he mocked Casey: "I still think I won. I have hurt you. I have killed your friends and taken them away from you. Nothing you can ever do will bring them back. I have won!" Montfort reached over to slap him across the mouth to shut him up. But before his hand could reach Mtuba's face, Casey's own scarred hand grabbed Mtuba by his neck. Jerking him bodily out of his seat, he hurled him out the open door. Casey looked down at the wildly flailing arms and legs as Mtuba fell three thousand feet to land headfirst on the hard, sun-baked veldt.

"Why did you do that?" Montfort yelled at Casey.

Casey looked Montfort straight in the eye, giving the major the distinct feeling that someone had just walked over his grave.

"Let's just call it a love offering, Major. That's all, just an offering." Van and Harrison had to lean next to his mouth to hear his next words, they were spoken so softly.

"Let's go home now. I'm very tired."

THE ETERNAL MERCENARY
By Barry Sadler